JANIE BLUE

DEBUT NOVEL BY SUZY ACCOLA

THE IDEA BOUTIQUE®

Publisher: Lisa M. Burwell
Editor/Proofreader: The Idea Boutique® – Jordan Staggs
Proofreader: Margaret Stevenson
Literary Consultant: Hunter Burgtorf
Interior layout and cover design: The Idea Boutique® – Sally Neal

PUBLISHED BY

THE IDEA BOUTIQUE®

An imprint of Cornerstone Marketing and Advertising, Inc.

ISBN: 978-0-9989149-4-7 (PRINTED VERSION)
ISBN: 978-0-9989149-5-4 (E-BOOK VERSION)

Library of Congress Control Number: 2023908616

To my husband, Jim, who makes every day an adventure and loves me with my flaws and all—how fun life is with you in it!

Maddie, Sammi, and Carson (my kiddos): your wit, resilience, spirit, and friendship inspire and lift me up daily! You have the innate ability to connect and undoubtedly are change makers.

Wilde, my sweet Aussie, your loyalty, endless energy, and kisses make me smile inside and out.

You are ALL the BEATS to my HEART. I love you. xoxo

JANIE BLUE

By

Suzy Accola

Chapter 1

DOUBLE TAKE

T he gray light through the window caught her attention. Trickling rain persisted with fog so thick you could slice it with a bay-onet. With that, Ella jolted out of her warm, soft blankets and sat upright. She took a deep breath, soaking in the soothing colors of her bedroom while focusing on tiny reflections dotting the ceiling above. She sighed, then marched herself into the dimly lit bathroom. Tentatively switching on the light, Ella moved closer to the mirror with bloodshot, blue eyes inspecting her dark circles with the faintest of lines forming at the corners. Squinting at her reflection, she sighed at neglected skin and stringy, lifeless black hair. Hmm . . . She was relieved at the moment that the oval mirror was on the small side and showed only from her chest up. Her thirtieth birthday would be rough this spring if she did not start taking care of herself. Today was going to be a day of renewal. She would climb out of this depression, kick herself in the ass, and regain a winning attitude. Or at least fake it. As the sheets of rain sounded outside, it was not the best start . . .

Looking back into the mirror, she said, "Ella Carmichael, today you will be the person you were always meant to be." She had begrudgingly finished reading Chapter 1 of a new self-help book entitled *Get Out of Bed*. John, the author, said to repeat something positive about yourself every day at least ten times and out loud. After seeing her reflection, she could hardly say with conviction, "Ella, you are beautiful inside and out." Besides, she really needed to get in touch with her inner self. Maybe a yoga class would inspire her or at least ease her into the morning. The soft yoga pants and layered Lululemon tanks seemed like an extension of pajamas.

Dan, Ella's husband, woke up early to leave for work. She heard his chirping alarm go off at 4:45 a.m. and pretended to be out cold. Politics could be so cutthroat, and he was riding in the fast lane up to the Hill. Ella could see the stress on his face every time he looked at her as his jaw muscles clenched. She was certain he was wondering if she would be the end of his bright career. Secretly, she hoped he failed miserably and found himself in a dark cell one day.

The night before, he commented that she needed to try and find a hobby or interest to reignite her winning attitude. It was funny how he continually used phrases to benefit his rise to the top. Obviously, her semblance of stability and grace played a major factor in whether or not Dan Carmichael would officially be on the ballot for senator in the 2000 election next year. She knew that was probably the reason he married her in the first place. She looked and acted the perfect part of a potential first lady—at least before the accident. He used to joke that Ella looked so much like a young Jackie O, they could have been sisters.

Looking at the ground instead of Dan, Ella breathed in through her small, straight nose. Just as she let her breath out slowly, she cocked her head to one side and met his anxious and irritated green eyes.

Quietly, but firmly, she said, "I'll try, Dan. Life has given me a few lemons lately. It's going to take a lot more than sugar and water to make the sweet lemonade you like."

With that, Dan awkwardly kissed her smooth cheek. In reaction to his movement toward her, Ella defensively crossed her arms in front of her chest and felt her body tense. He pursed his lips together into a straight line, looking like he might have been biting his cheek. She waited for him to say something to give away his true feelings or suspicions. Instead, he just sniffed the air, rolled his eyes, and went back to his office to work on another blue-ribbon speech.

It had been two weeks since she lost the baby. She blamed Dan. Denying her hatred for him was perhaps the hardest thing she'd ever done. As lost and tired as she felt, Ella was a survivor. At least she felt *something*. She would not turn into one of those women who crawl back into bed every day until one day they just don't get up at all.

On the surface, most women would think her undeniably blessed. She was married to a great-looking, successful man. As a politician with a rising career, he always seemed to say the right thing for the press. Therefore, he seemed the perfect man. As icing on the cake, she was drop-dead gorgeous and had a spot on the board of a high-profile charity with her name on it. If anyone took the time to look below the calm, lovely waters, they would see how appearances could be very deceiving. An icy chill looming over dark, rough waters tore a wind tunnel through reality.

The concoction of Zoloft and Propranolol for her post-traumatic stress disorder lay on the counter for her to take. For such an uncaring asshole, it was funny how Dan had not forgotten every day for the past six weeks to incessantly remind her to take her meds. As usual, he watched her take them. When he left the room, she pulled them from her pajama sleeve and flushed them down the toilet.

It was breakfast time, but food was the furthest thing from her mind. Coffee, yes, but the thought of much more than that made her nauseated. In fact, for the past couple of months, Ella would wake up, make a piece of toast with butter, and methodically chew and swallow until it was gone. Afterward, she would sip her coffee, breathing in the slight aroma of vanilla. Finally, begrudgingly, she would start her day.

The past two weeks, however, she just went back to bed.

Today was not one of those days, she told herself.

Shivering, Ella turned up the heat. Hoping to warm the chills, she decided to take a long, hot shower. She shampooed her hair twice, used a deep, minty conditioner, and left it on while she shaved her legs. Afterward, Ella slathered her body with almond body butter. She'd forgotten how good it felt to have a pampering routine. She stepped out of the shower feeling both invigorated and relaxed. Her robe felt soft and cozy as she sat down at the vanity and dried her hair. With a little gel and a lot of pulling, her thick, naturally wavy locks were straight, smooth, and shiny. Next, she rubbed in some moisturizer, brushed bronzer onto her cheeks and forehead, added a touch of mascara to her long lashes, and dabbed on nude-colored lip gloss. She carefully chose slimming black flared yoga pants, thick socks, a tank, a cozy Lucky sweatshirt, and a slightly wrinkled khaki trench coat. She slipped on her favorite Birkenstock slides and felt a small surge of energy.

With that, Ella smiled and decided that, rain or shine, she *needed* coffee to get started on this venture out. She didn't mind the rain on her face or windshield. Dreary weather rarely affected her mood; it was just part of the charm the Pacific Northwest had to offer. After pulling her dark-blue Land Rover into the parking lot and heading into the warm coffeehouse, she quietly walked up to the mahogany counter and saw that the owner's back was to her.

Matter-of-factly, she ordered, "Caffe latte, no foam, please. Sir, can you make that extra hot?"

Delighted at the sound of her voice, Frank happily spun around and laughed heartily at Ella. She knew he'd be surprised and wanted to ease the tension with laughter. Frank couldn't help grinning as he saw a genuine smile turning up on his favorite customer's face. She had been MIA from his coffeehouse for months.

He simply said, "How nice it is to see you and your infectious smile again, Ella. Looks like the real deal."

She wanted to say more and considered half joking that her husband was keeping her prisoner, but knew her words could be overheard and end up in the papers taken out of context. Instead, she flashed Frank another small, sweet smile and politely added that she missed him and his famous lattes, promising not to be so scarce in the future.

After doctoring up her latte, Ella walked out the door feeling a little lighter. There was even a hint of sunlight peeking through the clouds. In her daydreamy state, Ella barely noticed the tall, blond, unshaven man who bumped into her, spilling the perfect latte all over her coat.

He looked as if he'd seen a ghost, but then he picked her up and quietly exclaimed, "My God, it's really you! Janie Blue, where the hell have you been? I thought you were gone."

Confused and flustered, Ella stuttered, "Ex-c-use m-e, you definitely have me mixed up with someone else. Besides, that's a lousy way to apologize for splattering my drink everywhere."

Happiness and fear gripped Ella. She could not look him in the eyes, or she would do one of two things: fall to the ground or fall straight into his arms.

She thought frantically, "How could he be alive, standing in front of me? Who had followed him here? How long would he stay alive if anyone saw him with me? Who else would we put in danger by talking?"

The man—she didn't even dare to *think* his name, lest she fall apart—was intensely good-looking in a Calvin Klein model meets outlaw Jesse James sort of way. Suddenly, Ella was keenly aware of people staring, so she started walking toward her Land Rover.

He kept pace with her, adding angrily, "Is this for real, Janie? All of this? Amnesia and a good-girl act? I know you could never understand why I left you in the state you were in, but let me explain."

"Listen, I don't know who you think you are, but clearly you have me confused with someone else." Shaking with anger and nerves, she looked him straight in the eyes and calmly told him, "Let go of my arm. Your nails are digging trenches into my skin, which might cause me to scream in about three seconds."

The man let go and started to back away, but *knowing* it was Janie, he quickly threw a round plastic coin toward her face—a test. She did not disappoint him. Without hesitation, her hand instinctively and fluidly caught the object before it hit her doll-like visage.

In a state of controlled anger and through clenched teeth, Ella said, "Sir, you are having a bad day, and I certainly don't need your charity."

She carefully handed him his hundred-dollar poker chip. In doing so, she brushed her fingers against his palm, and he gently cupped her hand in his. Instantly, she felt her breath taken away.

Just then, Matt, a local man in uniform, distracted Ella as he waved from across the parking lot and started heading in her direction. She worried he had noticed the guy professing to know her as someone else. She turned to see what the blond man was going to say, but he had disappeared. At least she did not see him intently studying her from the car he slipped into.

Still flustered, Ella stammered, "So, uh, Matt, how has Katie been lately? Please tell her I've just been so busy with thank-you notes and . . ."

"No need to explain, Ella. Dan has been filling us in. Do you know that guy you were talking to?"

"Uh, no, not at all. He accidentally spilled my drink on me and was trying to give me some money for a dry-cleaning bill. It was a nice gesture, but I really just want to go home and change at the moment," she said without hesitation. She was getting damn good at covering up her feelings.

Matt did not want to bother her and quite frankly was uncomfortable with the idea of a potential touchy-feely talk about the loss of her mother or her miscarriage. Instead of broaching any off-limits subjects, he awkwardly told her it was nice seeing her out and about again.

"Nice to see you again, too, Matt. Take care."

Matt nodded and gave a little wave back with the understanding that neither he nor she wanted to engage in small talk. Ella got the feeling that everyone was tiptoeing around her as if she were a fragile china doll that may break at any given moment. With one more anxious, desperate look around for Chase—*Chase*, she finally thought—Ella quickly stepped into her car. Gripping the steering wheel tightly, she took off. Once out of sight from anyone at the coffeehouse, she pulled over in front of the deserted Old Mill House down the road. She covered her face with shaking hands and let the tears stream down her cheeks. For the past two months, she thought Chase, the man she believed to hold her very soul, had been murdered. Thank God she had not been taking the pills, or she would have thought she'd been hallucinating seeing him just now. But how was this possible?

Elated and frightened at the same time, Ella had to resume her day as normal. Certain that people were watching her, she managed to move forward with her morning. She decided to get a massage so that she could be alone without any suspicions. It would be quiet on the island on a weekday. Perhaps she would even check out the shipping lines on the Sound if the sun stayed out. This way, she could breathe, think, and plan.

Earlier, Dan had said, "Ella, just relax and really enjoy yourself *all day long*. But, please, get out of the house."

So be it, then. She'd stay out of the house for a few hours to keep him from looking at her with annoyance and pity. She hesitantly booked a massage from her Nextel phone after she parked in front of Cielo's, an eclectic store filled with Italian-made clothes and unique gifts. Usually, Mara, the owner, offered fantastic Italian cookies and sodas to her clients. The shop music was a mix of Italian classics and old show tunes, depending on the season or the time of day. She perused the shelves for a little while, killing time before her appointment, but enjoying any sense of normalcy seemed impossible after her run-in with a ghost.

Ella had to find a way to contact Stacey, her best friend, without raising any alarms to the surveillance team. Concocting a plan occupied her thoughts for most of her "relaxing" spa treatment, but at least it kept her mind off *him*.

She was physically and emotionally drained by the time she reached the top of the stairs to her home a few hours later and opened the heavy, chic industrial steel door. Her thoughts had inevitably refocused on Chase, but she needed to keep her emotions in check. She decided to text Stacey: "Thank you for asking, but I have a follow-up doctor's appointment today at three." She hoped her friend would understand the meaning and meet her at the hospital to talk.

Ever since the incident in Las Vegas, her doctor had prescribed these little yellow-orange pills for her with explicit directions, stating, "Ella, you cannot fail to take your pill every morning at the same time, with or without meals. This type of injury will not heal without these."

No one understood the cause of her amnesia after the car accident, even herself. But for Ella, it became the only way out of a very bad situation. Life or death. When told to take her pills, she did not question the doctor—nor did she obey him. One thing about this "trauma" pill was that it was compared to a memory inhibitor in an article she read. It seems our memories are like Jell-O, and this drug could suppress them while the memories are in the setting stage. Wanting all her *new* memories to stay intact, Ella took great pains to avoid taking this pill or any others. She became a master magician in the art of feigning pill popping.

Because the meeting with Stacey was not for three hours, she decided to lie down. This had been a big day for Ella, and sleep came quickly. As she drifted off, she dreamed she was lovingly and playfully looking at a man. In fact, he was playing a magic trick on her and pulled a deck of cards from behind her ear. While picking a card, she laughed easily as if she'd known him forever. In return, he effortlessly picked her up as if to kiss her. Suddenly, they were apart like the page of a book torn down the middle. The tear looked like the letter *Y*, and the cards slowly flew into the air.

It was all in slow motion until her eyes flew wide open. She needed to catch her breath. Each moment was a memory; each breath brought her closer to the truth.

Chapter 2

NINE WEEKS EARLIER

Finality often occurs without closure or consolation. The tragic death of Ella's mother left her with so many incomprehensible feelings. Her mother was only sixty years old. One day she was nagging Ella about her responsibilities as a politician's wife and pushing her to have a child before thirty. She was sure it was the public's perception that her and Dan's marriage appeared weak without any children. The next day, her mother was gone. She had a heart attack at home by herself while cooking her famous coq au vin. She didn't even have a chance to call 911.

When Ella's father, Mike, found his wife's body lying on the floor, she had been dead for an hour and forty-five minutes. The chicken was perfectly cooked when he mindlessly took it out of the oven, as if she had timed it that way. She was so organized that in her will she asked to be cremated so as to delay the service until it could be "properly organized." Mike also knew she had wanted her ashes floating in the waters near Balboa Island in California, where she had grown up. That's where Ella came in. Her mother raised her to be a gracious hostess. Quietly and patiently, she prepared everything perfectly for every party or event, leaving no detail forgotten. Of course, she, with some help from her aunt, would be the one to arrange the memorial.

Ella found her grief so surreal and unexpected. The drive from their home in the state of Washington to her aunt's house in California would give her the time she desperately needed to sort out feelings, cry to sad songs, or listen in silence, hoping to find a sign to make sense of this chaos. Thank God her dad was holding up. He was like a treasure chest: very tough and solid on the outside, but once inside, you found amazing delights. He was a softie at heart with those he loved, and he could be pretty funny in his own way. He always comforted Ella as a child by making her laugh when she felt like crying. He and Ella had their own secret language, which her mother found seriously annoying. Ella caught her winking at her father once, though, when she thought Ella wasn't looking. She wished she had known that lighthearted side of her mom, but she could never seem to crack the code. She was always standoffish, yet fiercely protective of Ella and keeping their lives private.

Dan, Ella's husband, would not be joining her for the drive down to Aunt Ceci's. His schedule was intense at work. He seemed so intent on moving up the political ladder that he could barely feign sadness about her mother's death. He told Ella how proud he was of her for staying strong and that she should focus her energies on creating a beautiful memorial. As if on cue, he reminded her that hopefully, one day soon, they'd be in Washington, D.C., instead of Washington State. Surely, that was one of the reasons Dan married her. She looked and acted like a perfect politician's wife. He could always trust her to do and say the "right" thing.

She was not sure if it was a specific moment or what exactly triggered her growing dislike of Dan. They had been married for three years, and more and more, it seemed he cared only for himself. It was the way he consistently satisfied himself first in every way. Even when they had a big night out, he would make sure he was dressed perfectly, holding his Scotch in hand before he even attempted to pour her a glass of wine. Lately, he seemed to open her car door only when he knew they'd be seen. Of course, during those times "in the spotlight," he was the perfect gentleman. Ella was surprised he hadn't pushed her about having a child. They had tried, but every time she got excited at the thought she may be pregnant, only one pink line appeared on the stick's window.

One night, Ella asked Dan, "How many children would you like?"

"Ella, if you are able to have them, I guess a couple would be good."

Ella thought about this carefully but didn't say anything. She wondered if he thought something was wrong with her, that she couldn't conceive a child. Maybe there was an issue there, and soon she would check into it. She also couldn't shake the feeling that he couldn't care less. Who says, "I guess a couple would be good," as if they were discussing apples at the grocery store?

After staying with her father for a couple of days, Ella had repacked her red floral Lilly Pulitzer duffel bags and was preparing for the long drive to Southern California. She glanced around for her father and found him leaning against her mother's favorite redwood tree. It was majestic and graceful, just like she had been. Mike was slowly caressing the bark and smiling at something. She didn't want to interrupt him but wanted to get going so she could maximize the daylight driving time. Night driving made her nervous, especially when she didn't know her route well.

Ella quietly approached her dad, saying, "I know you miss her, Dad. So do I. You seem mesmerized by her favorite tree."

"She loved this tree, and let me tell you why. Of course, it is beautiful, but look over here, Ella."

He pointed to a small fanned-out heart with the letters *K E M* etched into the trunk. "Do you remember the wonderful picnic we had by the lake the first day we moved here? Your mother was so happy and carved all our initials in this tree. When she finished the last line in the *M*, she proclaimed it was good luck. Although she pretended not to be superstitious, I know for a fact that she would never walk under a ladder and would cry if she broke a mirror."

He had a tear in his eye but was smiling too. "Ella, I know you felt Mom was tough, overprotective, and a bit cold, but she wasn't always that way. She loved you with all her heart. To her, this tree represented our family, and this is where she came to think, pray, and find peace."

Ella wasn't sure what to say about this side of her mother she hardly knew. She smiled sadly and told her dad she needed to get on the road so as to make it to Eugene before dark. As Ella headed for her car, her father looped his arm through hers and steered her in a different direction, heading back toward the house for an unexpected surprise.

Chapter 3

THE ROAD LESS TRAVELED

E lla decided not to object and quietly walked along with him. When they reached his workshop with the extra garage attached, he opened up the sliding barn doors to reveal her mother's old MG. Only now, it had been completely restored to its former shiny, bumblebee yellow with a new black convertible top. He handed her a chunky key hanging on a dated, bright-yellow smiley face keychain.

Mike whispered, "Care to ride her down to your aunt's?"

At this, Ella could no longer hold back the tears.

In an effort to lighten the mood, she laughed while wiping the moisture from her cheeks and reminded him, "Dad, you do realize I haven't driven Mom's car since I was sixteen, very tipsy, and going for a joy ride with Stacey, my 'wild' friend, as you called her back then?"

"Yes, Ella, but you are all grown up, married, and responsible. I don't think I've seen you have much more than a glass of wine since that day. If you can handle being the wife of a politician and your mother's funeral preparation, you can certainly take on this little car.

Besides, I seem to remember your love of go-carts—which led me to teach you to drive a stick shift in the first place. You took to it like a natural-born race-car driver and never popped the clutch." He laughed. "In fact, the only way I could talk your mother into allowing you to go drive the go-carts was by explaining the importance of learning defensive driving skills. She never knew how fast I'd let you fly around that track."

With tears streaming down her face, she hugged him until he could barely breathe.

He laughed. "Ella, sweetie, you're still the best hugger around. Now, Aunt Ceci is expecting you by late Wednesday afternoon. I made a list of some good hotels along the way. I'll be down to help with any final arrangements." He sighed. "I wish we could bury her on our property, but you know it's always been her wish to be cremated and have her ashes taken out to the California coast where she grew up and we first met. It was such a special place for her."

"I know, Dad."

"Drive safely, honey. I love you."

As she put the MG in gear and headed down the highway, a sense of peace filled her. She managed the gears well. She had forgotten how much fun it was to drive a stick shift. It brought her back to her childhood and teen years. Her father had even sweetly left an envelope on the passenger seat labeled "For Gas" with some cash in it, knowing she would have refused if he tried to offer it to her in person.

A few hours into her road trip, Ella felt like she could breathe freely for the first time in a long time. Deciding to take the back road seemed like a great idea and reminded her of another time long ago. The scenery mimicked the melancholy nostalgia she was feeling. She turned up the radio and let the pavement disappear beneath her wheels.

The Beatles' song "In My Life" was playing as Ella's mind drifted through so many of her memories with her family. She could never seem to remember any important event or time with her parents before kindergarten. Perfectly natural, though, she thought, as who really does remember anything significant at such a young age? Even the deer running alongside the road seemed to agree. She was loping along to the music as well. It was mesmerizing—until another deer appeared out of the trees and zigzagged. In a single, fleeting moment, it leaped across the road in front of the car.

"This is not going to happen! I am not going to hit a deer in my mother's car just three days after she died, dammit!" Ella screamed.

Swerving to avoid the deer, she lost control. In an instant, the little MG was bouncing through the woods as trees flew by in all directions. Then, with a loud scratching sound, everything stopped, and her head was slammed hard against the wheel. There was only darkness.

Some say in complete darkness, we fear the unknown or that which we cannot see. Or maybe what we fear is the possibility of exposing something that already exists in ourselves. Once the inevitable occurs, there may not be a place to go back to that we can happily call home. Ella felt as if she were drifting away and would never be the same again. In fact, when she came to, "Ella" loomed somewhere in the distance, and her mind let another personality take control as if shifting into overdrive.

Chapter 4

JANIE WHO?

"**O**uch!" Her head was throbbing as she came to, cursing with a Southern drawl, "What the hell is going on here? Did some trucker run me off the road? My head is bleeding like the Mississippi."

Janie found a first-aid kit in the glove compartment and put a large, square bandage on her head, barely noticing that the large bump was swelling. Next, she stepped out of the MG. She walked around the car and didn't see too much damage. A window had been broken, and a large tree limb was in its place. That must've been what had knocked her out. There was also a large dent in the door and a slight rip in the canvas top. Not too bad, she thought. Hopping back in the slightly beat-up MG, she started the engine. It seemed to work just fine, at least. She decided there was no need for a window anyway—or a top, for that matter—and manually rolled it down. She couldn't wait to get on the road, crank some tunes, and feel the wind in her hair. Her mama always told her "Fun" was her middle name. In fact, there was a certain pillow fight she could remember having with her mama when she was no more than four years old. After a lot of laughter and giggling, all of the feathers wound up floating in the air and settling on the furniture and floor. Janie forced her mom to surrender by tickling her. She was then given the nickname Janie "Fun" Blue.

For now, Ella's memories were locked away, and Janie took the wheel.

She changed the station to KROQ, pulled out the bobby pins holding her hair in a tight French twist, and, one by one, tossed them out of the car. As she revved the engine and put the car into reverse, she knew it would be a day to remember. Not only did the tires bump over more broken branches, but somewhere in the wake lay her cracked and broken phone. As soon as the car hit the road, she quickly worked the gears from reverse to first, second, third, and fourth as fast as they would go.

She turned up the stereo volume full tilt and sang at the top of her lungs, "Out here in the fields, I fight for my meals. I get my back into my living. I don't need to fight to prove I'm right. I don't need to be forgiven. Yeah, yeah, yeah, yeah, yeah," and drove as fast as she could toward a place she used to call home as a little girl.

After driving for most of the night and making two nondescript stops for gas, the oil light came on. It was only nine in the morning and already hot enough to fry eggs. Janie remembered trying that as a child and being fascinated that it really worked. Just then, smoke started billowing out from under the MG's hood.

She murmured, "Oh shit! What do I do now?" and pulled over at the next exit, consisting of two run-down buildings. One of them was a gas station—sort of. At least there was an old, unused gas pump and a sign saying, "Be back at 2:00" on the door. She wondered just how reliable that was.

The place looked a bit abandoned. Janie decided to sit down on a plastic milk crate and enjoy the desert sun beating down upon her while waiting for the owner to show up. It was as quiet as a ghost town on the side of this dusty Nevada highway.

She stretched her arms in the air and yawned with her mouth wide open, now realizing how exhausted she was from driving all night. Her hair looked wildly tousled and wavy from the convertible. Her normally pale skin was starting to look tanned, with faint specks of freckles. At the last gas station, she had found a red bandana to cover the now noticeable goose egg on her head and had bought a vintage Rolling Stones tee. She could not handle the uptight and itchy blouse she'd been wearing. At least the dark blue jeans were comfortably tight and flattering. Besides, she thought, "Jeans need an old T-shirt like peanut butter needs jelly on a sandwich."

Not ten minutes after she pulled over, just as beads of sweat started forming on her skin, a man drove up in a tricked-out silver Jeep. He looked like he was ready to take a ride through the desert in this car. At first, he did not look thrilled to come to her aid—until he got a closer look. He flashed her a crooked smile while brushing his messy, sun-streaked hair out of his face, unveiling serious Paul Newman eyes.

She called out to him happily, thinking he must be the owner of the place, "Am I glad to see you! I thought you'd never show up!"

Looking at her overheated car and grease-smudged face, Chase let out a sexy laugh. "I am not Joe of Joe's Auto, but I'm sure not going to let a beautiful lady wait here alone or dehydrate until he shows up. Would you care for a drink, miss . . .?"

"It's Janie, Janie Blue. And, yes, just about anything will do at the moment."

"Well, Miss Blue, my name is Chase, and I can offer you a slightly lukewarm beer and see if I can't help you with your car until your guy Joe here decides to show up."

He grabbed a beer and tossed it to her a little fast, but Janie's reflexes were on fire, and she caught it easily. Her throat was so dry it ached. In less than ten seconds, she caught the glass bottle, twisted off the cap, and gulped it down before saying in her sweet Southern drawl, without sarcasm, "Why, thank you, Chase. You are a true gentleman."

He certainly didn't expect that coming from this petite beauty. In an effort to impress her, he lifted the hood of the MG to assess the damage. Right away, Chase whistled and explained, "I can't fix this baby without replacing some parts." He wondered how far she'd driven it in this sorry state.

"Listen," he said, "I'll have a beer and play a game or two of blackjack with you until Joe gets here to open up the place."

This guy seemed nice enough, Janie thought; he was certainly good-looking and funny. So far, she did not suspect him to be a rapist or serial killer. On another note, he also wasn't going to steal her car.

He grabbed another Corona for each of them and got out two packs of playing cards. While downing another beer, Janie watched Chase shuffle the deck.

During his second shuffle, Janie giggled sarcastically as she asked, "While I may seem gullible, I know a deck of cards is 52. We have two decks, so why are there 108 cards?"

"How the hell did you count those while I shuffled?" asked Chase.

She surprised herself, as she didn't know how she'd done it, but was pleased by her newfound quick wit and perceptiveness. "I'm pretty sure I have a photographic memory or might even be a math genius."

This information seemed hilarious to her as she exploded into infectious laughter, and Chase could tell that she was really loosening up from the two beers. Still, now he was not sure whether she was sent by the casino boss's buddies to set him up, so he threw a couple of tests her way. Not only did she pass them, but it was enough to intrigue him into hanging around this very sexy, quirky woman. Perhaps her skills could come in handy when he decided to outwit and impress the next casino.

Minutes turned into an hour, and finally, Chase said, "I am going around back to check for myself when ol' Joe might be coming back."

As he walked around to the side door, he saw a second sign below "Be back at 2:00" lying facedown and dusty on the ground. He turned it over, reading, "Gone fishin'. Will bring back the bass

June 2nd." That was almost two weeks from today.

He returned to Janie with the news, cracked his cute, crooked smile, and stated in a monotone voice, "Dear Jane, I cannot leave you here for two weeks waiting for some crazy redneck to take advantage of you."

"What are you saying?"

He held up the dirty sign, and they both burst out laughing.

"Really," Chase said, "at least I can take you one stop closer to your destination, which is . . .?"

"Vegas, of course," she answered. As she stumbled to her car, Janie mumbled, "Let me grab my purse." She was a little unsure of accepting a ride from Chase but was definitely more afraid of being stranded here. She couldn't think of a soul to call. In fact, she felt very fuzzy and a little dizzy—probably from the beer, the heat, and the lack of food, she reasoned.

In her intoxicated state, she didn't even notice when her wallet— well, Ella's wallet—slipped out of her purse and fell under the seat.

Keeping it light and trying to sound cheery, she smiled and said, "Okay, I'm all ready for fun! Let's kick this dust bucket!"

Chase had the good sense to move her car to the back of Joe's so as to deter anyone from stealing it. It's definitely off the beaten path, but someone might see the bright yellow MG and notice the fact that Joe was not around. As they hopped into his Jeep, he couldn't resist the urge to reach over so he could buckle her in tightly with a grin.

"Viva Las Vegas, Janie!"

Chapter 5

SANDS IN TIME

Follow bliss or careen toward the abyss. Contemplating both possibilities, Janie chose the former with conviction. As the Jeep headed toward the red desert hills away from the highway, she felt reborn. She was free to just *be*. They drove in silence for a while as the bumpy terrain made it awkward to talk. With sand flying in all directions, including toward her mouth, Janie hesitated to open it. Chase tossed her a pair of aviator sunglasses.

"You're gonna need these for the ride. I think you'll find this route quite interesting. Ever been through the desert off-road?"

Yawning, she replied, "No, can't say I have."

Sleep overtook her. Janie was unable to keep her eyes open. In minutes, she was out cold with a slight grin on her face. As Chase looked over at his welcome passenger, she appeared even prettier than when he first laid eyes on her. He hadn't wanted to take the main highway that would have gotten them to Vegas in a few hours. Instead, he decided to take the long route through the canyon and up over Red Rock. He was intrigued by Janie's willingness to come with him and the sheer coincidence that she was on his route just after he left his meeting with Marty, his liaison to Global Insurance. He needed to be certain of her story. Also, he did not want her to know the secret location of his trailer, so he was relieved she passed out—probably from the beer, the long drive, and the 105-degree heat. The mixture worked like a charm.

Just as Chase slowed down and put the Jeep into park, Janie woke up begrudgingly, squinting her eyes. Her mouth was dry, and her head ached. She felt a bit like she was maneuvering around the final stages of a dream—when everything is hazy and you cannot move quickly, even if someone is chasing you. Maybe water would have been a better beverage choice than beer.

Eyeing a silver Airstream in the middle of what looked like nowhere, Janie raised only one question: "Do you have toothpaste and water in that silver bullet?"

Chase could only imagine how she felt, so he obligingly let her in to use the toilet and grabbed a spare toothbrush and minty toothpaste, along with a bottle of cold water for her to clean up. It wasn't very often that he brought women here, but he liked to be prepared.

She spent five minutes washing her sand-blasted face, brushed her gritty teeth clean, and threw her incorrigible, wavy hair into a messy bun on top of her head. She decided to wash the filthy bandana and discard the bandage underneath. Her wound was now just a small cut surrounded by a swollen, bluish bruise. All in all, she felt okay. She really needed that rest and was pretty sure she had already slept like a log for a few hours.

"You clean up pretty good, but that's a nice shiner on your forehead. How did it happen?" Chase tilted his head at her as she emerged from the tiny bathroom.

"I got in a little fender bender on the way down, hence the dent in my car. No big deal, I just bumped my head. Really, I'm fine."

"Do you want to borrow a clean T-shirt? That one looks like it has seen better days."

In a mocking tone, she bantered back, "What are you talking about? I just bought this thing of beauty. It's vintage! I will admit, though, it's pretty grubby after that ride."

Chase grabbed a royal blue Cubs crewneck from his days growing up in Chicago. He turned his back toward her as she quickly changed. It took a lot of willpower for him not to peek. When he did turn, he couldn't help noticing how the bright blue in the shirt made her eyes shine. She really was a catch, he thought, and he wondered again just who she was and why she was here. This trip was not over yet by any means. He would definitely find out. His people skills were stellar, and he had a way of pulling information from them.

"Ready for an adventure, Janie?" he asked with a wink and slight nod.

Without really waiting for an answer, he grabbed what looked like a couple of sleeping bags and a brown paper bag of food. "I've got the rest of the necessities in the Jeep. Let's hit it. It gets dark early in the canyon."

Janie just shrugged her shoulders, smiled sweetly, and headed toward the car. It was a nice feeling just to go with the flow and let someone else direct traffic. Although Chase found it a bit odd that she wouldn't question him, nor did she seem the least bit afraid of being alone with a stranger at his trailer in the middle of the desert, he also found this enticing. It would be a challenge to uncover what secrets lay within this mysterious package.

Night fell within the hour. Soon there were beautiful huge red rocks surrounding them. They were now on a worn path where other off-road vehicles had ventured.

As they reached the vista, Chase jerked the Jeep into park and proclaimed, "We can stay here tonight. It's pretty treacherous going down, and I'd rather attempt it in daylight. I'll make us a little fire if that's okay with you. Also, I packed a couple of sandwiches, thinking this might happen."

Janie was barely listening as she looked up at the star-filled desert sky. "I'll bet you know all the constellations, too, Chase. I saw a small telescope in the back. Care to give me a lesson?"

"I do, and I would love to tell you all about the stars. Be careful, though . . . women tend to fall under my spell." He laughed.

She rolled her eyes but grinned as she continued to stare at the bright pinpoints in the blue-black sky.

By the time they finished the bottle of wine Chase also conveniently packed, he still had no information on her other than the fact that she was a great conversationalist. She asked very engaging questions and would always turn them around to get him talking. In fact, he found himself telling her stories of living in Chicago as a kid and working in a pool hall. It was tough not to fall for this one, he thought.

As she got up to grab a bottle of water from the car, Janie felt dizzy and tripped over a small rock. Chase caught her just before she fell forward on her face. He pulled her up toward him and, the proximity and wine getting the best of them, was about to kiss her. The wine, however, had not helped with Janie's potential concussion. She had the horrible urge to vomit, and she weakly pushed him out of the way before she ran behind a rock.

Hearing her heaving, Chase did not want to intrude but called out, "You okay over there?"

Barely audible, she mumbled, "Not really. I don't remember when I have felt worse." Chase felt a tinge of guilt for feeding her more wine without thinking about the goose egg on her head. While giving her space and waiting for her to emerge from behind the huge boulder, Chase found a large, flat rock on which to lay the sleeping bags and pillows. After a short while, Janie stumbled out from behind the rock, looking green. She managed a thin smile.

Sighing, she said, "I'm not sure I can say with confidence it'll stay down, but do you have any Tylenol? I feel as if I partied like a rock star and then got thrown out of the hotel headfirst through the window!"

"I've got something better than Tylenol for you. It's a secret remedy concocted by my buddy in Chicago. Works every time."

With that, he dropped an Alka-Seltzer into a beer and shook it up. Then, he added ginger ale. With her head to one side watching him, Janie looked at Chase with one eyebrow raised, smiled sardonically, and said simply, "I'll pass."

She lay down on the sleeping bag, holding her head, and fell to sleep. Her dreams were strangely surreal that night. Her recurring dream of a woman laughing while a child twirled around and around with her arms straight out like a helicopter seemed different than usual. Every other time, she could barely see the child's face and never the woman's. This time the dream was not blurred in the least. The child was definitely Janie, as she saw her wavy black hair and bright blue eyes and remembered the gap in her front teeth as she laughed. For the first time, the woman laughing appeared very clear. She looked so much like the little girl and looked at her with such love that Janie could see it was her mother. As the little girl fell to the ground from dizziness, her mother swooped down and picked her up in her arms. The burning questions in Janie's mind now were who was her mother and where was she now?

While Chase watched Janie sleep, he wondered what or who in her dreams made her laugh so sweetly. Again, he realized he knew nothing about her except that the more time he spent with her, the more his fascination grew. Nothing seemed to add up to anything, but maybe that was the point. Still, there was a reason she came in this direction; it was something compelling enough for her to leave her car behind and go off to Vegas with a stranger.

Chapter 6

ELIZA JANE

Absolutely, the best money comes in the evening. How Lizzie thought she could wait tables during the day while her daughter, Janie, was in school was beyond her. The tips were peanuts compared to what her friend Julia made at the Gentlemen's Club as a waitress. She wasn't sure about the skimpy outfit she would have to wear, but thought maybe the job as hostess would keep her at some distance from the grabby men. At least she would only greet, seat, and say goodbye to them. It seemed harmless enough.

Lizzie swept her bobbed, jet black, wavy hair away from her almost turquoise-blue eyes so she would be sure not to miss a step and trip into the Club for her interview. After many wardrobe changes, she and Jules decided the job would be hers for the taking if she wore the blue shift mini dress. The manager, Joe Handler, hired her on the spot after she lit up the room with her huge, innocent smile. He thought she would definitely bring the men in and hoped he would quickly move her into another, more adventurous role. She definitely came in a delectable package. The hair, doe eyes, fair skin, and tiny frame made her seem demure and very young. The men coming to the Club loved that idea.

"Lizzie, here's your outfit for tonight. Make sure you dazzle them with your smile, and don't forget to shake your ass when you walk them to their table. That'll get them enticed for the show and might possibly make you a few bucks. Hurry up, you have five minutes before we open."

Smiling with as much confidence as she could muster, Lizzie looked Joe straight in the eyes and said, "Sure thing, Mr. Handler. Thanks for the tip."

He knew this one could be a gold mine. She was adorable and polite. He also learned from Jules that she was pretty desperate for money. He'd be interested in saving her for himself.

As the weeks flew by, Lizzie became accustomed to her surroundings at the bar. The girls were friendly as she, in her role as hostess, was not yet their competition. Her tips were great, but the schedule was getting crazy. She barely saw Janie, her little girl. She was at preschool until two, and Lizzie started work at four. She came home in time to sleep four hours before Janie woke up for school. One hour in the morning and one after school did not seem right, but Lizzie was determined to make things work out in Las Vegas. There was no way she could crawl back to her family, who disowned her the day she made the decision to keep her baby.

She'd never forget her father yelling, "You are a disgrace to our family and to our church! Your life will be ruined by keeping that bastard child! You are on your own!"

The reality was that he wanted her to sell her baby and go to a place where no one would ever know she had a child. She was certain that he wanted the money, but he wanted it without taking any of the heat. How sad that Giji, her Grandma J, was not alive. With her around, everyone laughed. She was Southern with an Irish twinkle and spirit. She always told Lizzie that with her dark Irish looks came impulsive passion and a quick temper—two things she would need to rein in. Her pregnancy was definitely the result of unchecked, impulsive passion, she granted, and her temper was not quick but it was unforgiving. At her father's words, she quietly left the room. Later that evening, she packed her bags and left in search of a new life for herself and her unborn child. Five years later, it was 1975 and still no one had come looking for her. She never looked back.

Old, that was what Lizzie felt. She was twenty. Time was ticking, and life seemed to be a routine of work, work, work. That is, until she found the job at the Club. After she got over the initial shock of women parading around half-naked and the clientele being all men, she grew to like it. It was fun and lively, and her role was pretty subdued. She had not yet been subjected to anything too uncomfortable. Joe and the bouncers were quite protective yet still managed to keep their clients happy. One night, a regular had way too much to drink and cornered Lizzie in the coatroom. Everyone else was watching Jules and Serena dance the pole to "Lady Marmalade" by Patti Labelle. Luckily, Rocky, the toughest-looking bouncer with marine tattoos up and down his arms, was walking by just in time.

Out of the corner of his eye, he saw people in the coat area. When he peered into the room, Johnny McKay, a big spender, was grabbing Lizzie's arm and slurring.

Rocky yelled, "Hey Johnny, I think Serena's lookin' for you! Better hurry, before she starts talking with Don."

With that, Johnny, slightly angered and embarrassed, looked back at Lizzie and then walked away.

Flushed and nervous, she breathed out hard and said, "I owe you one, Rocky. You are my hero."

"That is payment enough, Lizzie. No girl has yet to call me a hero. Now, stay out of the coatroom when the show's goin' on."

Later that night, after leaving the Club and heading to her bus stop, Lizzie noticed a car following her. She got scared and started running to the covered space to catch the 19 to her house. In her adrenaline-wound state, she tripped on the curb and twisted her ankle, falling to the ground. She lay there in pain with a torn dress and bloody hands and knees. Out of nowhere, she saw a motorcycle heading toward her.

Chapter 7

CHANCE MEETING

Still on the pavement and shaken from her fall, Lizzie noticed drops of blood on her new pale-yellow sundress. Pushing her disheveled black hair from her eyes, she was perplexed and a little relieved to see the man on the motorcycle drive up. At that moment, the car she presumed was following her sped off.

"Billy, is that you?" she called to the motorcyclist.

"Yes, it is, and you look like you've seen a ghost, Lizzie. What got you so spooked, and how about a ride home? They may not let you on that bus with a torn dress and a broken heel, anyway," he half-joked. He watched her relax as he made light of her situation, and he thoroughly enjoyed helping her out.

Happily, she hobbled onto his Harley. Even in pain, she felt free and happy for a moment with the wind flying through her hair. She had definitely noticed Billy at the Club, but tried hard not to talk too much with the clients. He was about five-eleven and stocky with olive skin and dark, slicked-back hair, and he usually dressed in expensive suits. Tonight was an exception. He had on Levi's and a button-down shirt with a leather jacket. He did not wear a helmet, so she got to see the wave in his brown hair. It made him look years younger, maybe early thirties.

He helped her into her house and politely said, "I'd be happy to play the good doctor and tend to your wounds. Do you need any help?"

"I've had enough rescuing for the night, thank you."

"At your service. Good night, Lizzie. Take care of yourself."

Chapter 8

TOO GOOD TO BE TRUE

T he next day, at work, Lizzie could barely hobble fast enough to seat everyone at the Club. She knew she looked comical and was sure her boss would be upset and take away shifts she desperately needed to cover rent. How strange, she thought, that he smiled at her and said nothing derogatory. In fact, later that day a delivery came for her. She couldn't remember the last time she had received flowers. Maybe for her First Communion from Giji, her grandmother. Tonight was very different. She was presented with a dozen roses surrounding a cute Harley-Davidson bear sporting a big bandage around its leg. The card read, "When you're able to dance again, save one for me. Billy."

Billy was a well-respected regular at the Club. From what Lizzie noticed, he seemed to frequent it for meetings and admired yet stayed fairly clear of the women. He was always friendly and mildly flirtatious with her, although she had always been too busy to reciprocate. She knew she had found an influential friend or possibly more than that.

For a while, things were looking up for Lizzie. At work, the tips were far more generous due to Billy's influence on the clientele. Her boss was polite, and she was able to continue as a hostess and stay away from dancing. Although they were not yet an item, Billy acted possessive and protective of Lizzie. She was certain he spoke to Joe about keeping her in her current position while increasing her tips.

Getting into a groove makes everything easier. Lately, Lizzie genuinely smiled most of the time, and she laughed and relaxed with Janie in her off time. She felt a confidence that had been missing for a long time. Perhaps it was more financial stability mixed with the idea that someone truly cared for her.

Before working at the Club and meeting Billy, she constantly worried about money. Also, she never let anyone close to her. She was afraid they would find her boring, only to discard her as her parents had. On top of this, she did not want Janie to get attached to anyone who may be gone in a month's time.

At first, she and Billy seemed like a match made in heaven. He showed up every night she worked, lavishing her with expensive gifts. One day, she really wasn't sure whether to laugh or cry at the surprise left at the door for Janie to open.

After running to the sound of the doorbell, she screamed in delight, "Mommy, this is all I've ever wanted, and even Santa didn't bring her to me. Christmas isn't for thirty-eight more days! I love her! I love her!!!"

Already scooped up in her arms, Janie held a tiny, white Maltese puppy with a bright pink bow and a tag saying, "For Janie."

"Well, it does say she's yours, honey. I wonder who sent her to you?" as if she didn't know.

Lizzie could not help but smile at how happy this made Janie. What amazed her was the ability of a cute little puppy to bring on such a quick and loving bond. Her parents had never allowed her to have an animal, no matter how many strays she brought home. They would always take them to the local pound and say they didn't have room. She was not going to do anything like that to her daughter. "Cupcake" was there to stay, and Billy found a new way into both their hearts.

Later that evening after Janie fell asleep with Cupcake next to her, Lizzie wrapped her arms around Billy's neck, looked up into his eyes, and coyly yet sarcastically said, "You've completely ruined Christmas for us, Billy Martinelli. There will be nothing left to surprise us. Now Santa will come in and slip on the dog mess, never to return . . ."

"Not even a big, wet kiss from a mother who has just found the ultimate live toy to occupy her five-year-old and wear her out at the same time?"

"And then some." With that, he stayed the night and snuck out before Janie woke up.

Billy always knew just what she wanted or needed. Actually, it was quite uncanny how he seemed to know everything about her to the point of making her wonder if she were being watched. Was she? One day, she fibbed to get off work as she needed some time alone for herself. No work, kids, dogs, or men. Just Lizzie time. She dropped Janie off at the sitter's house with Cupcake and decided to give herself a spa night at home and watch *Gone with the Wind*. She had never had a chance to watch this classic.

Chapter 9

CONTROL FACTOR

D uring a scene in *Gone with the Wind* where Scarlett brushes off Rhett for Ashley again, the doorbell rang.

"Dammit," Lizzie muttered, "who's selling cookies at this time of night?" With her homemade avocado mask on her face and a robe on, she opened the door ready to say "Tonight, I cannot buy any." Instead, she shocked her boyfriend.

Billy laughed immediately, sarcastically saying, "I just wanted to drop something by in your mailbox, but saw the lights on and your silhouette through the curtains. Sorry to mess up your plans with Rose at the mall." He seemed happy that she was home.

She had forgotten the mask she had on her face and tried to explain, but he gave her a big kiss on the cheek and asked, "Are there any chips to go with the guacamole?"

As much as she wanted to finish *Gone with the Wind* before she had to return it to the video store, he made a tough case against the movie and got his way, as usual.

The next time Lizzie wanted to do her own thing did not turn out as well.

Her neighbor Renee had told Lizzie, "We never go out anymore, Liz. Let's have a girls' night out. I know weekends are crazy for you at work, so how about Tuesday? They have awesome tacos and great margaritas at Casa Mia down the street."

Her babysitter was free, she was off, and it seemed like a great idea at the time. What could be wrong with having a few drinks with a good friend? Apparently, Billy thought it was a very bad idea. When she came home later that evening, pretty tipsy after drinking one too many margaritas, Billy was waiting for her in her house. She saw him right away.

"Billy, what are you doing here?"

He had been watching her seemingly flirt with a guy at the bar and was furious. Without replying, he picked her up and literally threw her as hard as he could. Luckily, she fell against the couch, but "seeing stars" had a new meaning to her. Lizzie felt sick, not only from too many margaritas but also from seeing the guy she cared about act like a crazed caveman. She closed her eyes and fell unconscious.

Chapter 10

BALANCING ACT

When Lizzie came to a few minutes later, Billy had her in his arms, kissing her. Apologies flew from his mouth about his jealous insecurities, his bad temper, and having too much to drink. He promised he would make it up to her.

He never really did.

Just like George Strait sings, it's not the breaths we take but what takes your breath away that counts in life. Lizzie did not expect her last breath to come so soon. Billy was not changing for the better; he was becoming even more jealous and possessive. One minute he was so confident and the next he was absolutely paranoid.

Lizzie overheard her coworkers Francine and Margie whisper, "Looks like snow is falling in summer for Billy. He'll be downhill skiing and buying the lodge on top by the end of the month."

It upset her to think that Billy may be dealing coke, but more so that he may be using it. She tried hard to stay away from drugs and was absolutely against them if Janie was around. Although she'd noticed a lot of changes in him lately, she was sure Billy would soon figure out his issues and come around.

After all, she thought, he loved her and was too smart a businessman to get wrapped up in the very drugs he sold.

Something was definitely off, though. Their sex life had also been changing. Billy liked the usual role-playing, but nothing sadistic. She could deal with the cheerleader role or Playboy bunny fulfilling his every need, but bondage was where she had to draw the line. Sex and pain did not go together in her book. She thought she could trust him, but he took things too far. He asked her to allow him to tie her up. Hesitantly, she agreed. Billy used handcuffs instead of the loose scarves she would have expected. This made her a little nervous. He left the room without saying anything and left her locked to the antique iron headboard. After about five uncomfortable minutes, he returned with a strange, scary look in his eyes. After blindfolding her, Billy began to bind her feet and legs apart.

At this, Lizzie began to yell, "Nooo! I am done, Bi . . ." He did not let her finish her sentence as he put masking tape on her mouth. Just taking off his pants, Billy did not work his usual foreplay magic. Instead, he entered her fast and hard over and over until he decided to try choking her. One of the hookers had shown him this, and it had turned him on when he was really high. He went so far that Lizzie passed out. He thought he had killed her and freaked out, calling her name over and over until she woke up. She knew she could no longer trust Billy and was uncomfortably sore and bruised for a week thereafter. Mentally, she would not be able to think of sex in the same way again.

Billy had hurt her only that one time before when she had lied to him about going out with a friend so as not to hurt his feelings. Of course, he was dramatically apologetic afterward.

He got on his knees and pleaded, "Lizzie, this will never happen again. I love you too much and know I need to control myself."

She received extravagant presents every day for a solid week. She always wore the white gold Rolex with the opal face to remind him of that night.

He said, "I was saving this for your birthday, but I need to make amends with you any way possible, Lizzie. Please forgive me."

No gift would ever make her forget or forgive him. She was too scared to leave him now. Lizzie thought she'd better just accept everything he gave her and try to get back to what they had before. She decided to do a little detective work and find out what was really going on with him. Apparently, hinting to the bouncer, Rocky, was the wrong move.

Billy was really acting out of it that evening in particular, so Lizzie quietly walked up to Rocky to ask if he had any blow from Billy as she was tired and didn't think she'd make it through the night.

He looked at her strangely and said, "Sure, Liz, anything for you. Give me a minute."

He came back with an eight ball and asked with concern, "You sure you know what you're doing, Lizzie? Just didn't seem like your sort of thing."

Lying through her teeth with a sarcastic smile, she told him, "There is a first time for everything, but not this. Don't worry about little ol' me. You are right, though, Rocky. It's not my usual thing. Can we keep this quiet?"

"Just you and me, Lizzie. In fact, did I even see you tonight?"

"It's nice to know I can trust someone around here to watch my back." And she blew him a kiss to leave a lasting impression.

The impression was so strong that he would see it while getting beaten up within inches of his life later that evening by one of Billy's entourage for giving Lizzie drugs.

As Lizzie went home that evening, she had no idea what awaited her. She was sick to her stomach about the reality of Billy being a dealer and probable user, but thought she had a handle on the situation. He called the Club just before she left, saying she'd need to get a ride home as he was busy. This set off a bit of a red flag, but Lizzie thought he was working on another deal or was too looped to drive.

Although she was exhausted, she couldn't wait to kiss Janie good night. She always woke up so softly and said, "Cupcake and I love you to the moon, Mama," and would fall right back asleep.

Tonight would not be the same. As she turned the door handle, something felt different. In fact, she wasn't sure if it was even locked. Usually, Carla, her babysitter, would be asleep on the couch, but not this night. Billy was standing in the dark with a crazed look in his eyes. She'd never seen that look before on him and wanted to turn around and run. But she could not leave Janie.

She thought, "Where is Janie? Oh my God!!"

About three feet away from Billy lay Cupcake.

She looked distorted, as if her neck had been twisted around. She was lifeless. She was dead, and Lizzie was certain it had been Billy's doing. All Lizzie could think of was Janie.

Trying to sound strong, she planned to yell. In unfathomable fear, her voice was shaking as she stammered, "God damn you, Billy, where is my daughter? Get out of this house. I never want to see you again, you piece of shit!

He smiled in a drug-induced state and looked straight through her. This made her feel certain he had gotten to Janie, and she'd never felt so strongly about killing someone. She ran fast at him with all of her strength, swinging, punching, and kicking, but he swung her around and used a strong headlock move.

"Do you want your neck to look like that stupid dog's? You're too pretty for that. Perhaps I should just shoot you for butting into my business and hanging all over that bouncer at work."

At that, Lizzie kicked backward and hit him right in the kneecap with a lot of force. Billy screamed, which pissed him off so much that he threw her to the ground, ready for a fight. Lizzie's head hit the edge of the brick fireplace. He hoped to only to scare her into complete submission, but his plan backfired.

"Lizzie, Lizzie, get up, you bitch, and fight!" Billy said, shaken.

Lizzie saw something around the corner. Without moving her

body or eyes, she knew it was Janie. Thank God! She wanted to tell her she loved her, but instead asked Billy to come closer so she could tell him something. He bent down, not realizing to the full extent what was happening.

Lizzie did not want this man in Janie's life ever again. She definitely wanted him to get the hell out of her house, and she never wanted Janie to forget who he was. She pretended to whisper something, and took the wineglass from the hearth and quickly broke the stem free. Within an instant, Lizzie used all her strength to shove the sharp, rugged glass stem into Billy's cheek and scrape it deep through his flesh in a jagged motion. The effect looked like a bloody letter *Y* dripping down his cheek. He was so shocked he didn't know how loud he screamed, which got the attention of the neighbors.

Janie saw it all and froze. In the mind of a five-year-old, the bloody *Y* signified "Why?" She snapped out of it after a moment. By the time Janie ran to her mother, who was covered in her own blood and Billy's, Lizzie was gone, and so was Billy. Janie did not speak again for three months.

Chapter 11

WHERE TO?

Waking up is hard to do after a sleepless night preluding a looming hangover. Janie sat up on her elbows and winced in pain as the hot sun shone in her bloodshot eyes.

She quickly shut them again, held her head, and tried to roll her neck as she groaned, "Is it really time to get up?"

"Unless you want to fry in the sun on that rock! Besides, I have a meeting on the way to Vegas that I cannot miss. You gonna be okay in the car?"

After adjusting to the light, Janie was taken aback by the amazing view in daylight.

She took a deep breath, sucking in the thin morning desert air, and felt much better. "I'm game if you are."

Chase had already packed up the bags and managed to make cowboy coffee, where the coarse grounds sunk to the bottom after he poured hot water over them. Now, that smelled good to Janie. He offered her a stainless to-go mug.

"Nothin' like a strong cup of joe and saltine crackers to prepare you for the bumpy car ride. Just hit me in the arm if you can't take it, Janie."

Janie was grateful for the coffee and almost drank it down like water, knowing she would not be able to drink while driving through the desert in a Jeep.

Then she pointed to the crackers and said with a smirk, "I'll eat those in the car. I don't want to hold you up. Thanks for being such a great host."

With a grin on his unshaven face, he said, "Hop in, miss. Your chariot's awaiting."

They both jumped up into the silver Jeep at the same time and buckled in. Chase had gotten a text from Ray at the casino saying to stop by and pick up a note at the Pioneer Bar. He hesitated to take Janie to the infamous place owned by Billy, an ex-club owner who had a lot of connections to the casino industry's inner workings. However, it was one of the best "secret" bars just outside of Vegas and was rumored to be haunted.

"Where are we going? Anywhere interesting?"

He loved her naive, inquisitive interest. "You are in luck today. We're going to a haunted bar. It also has the best Bloody Marys in the West."

"That might just cure me or scare me into feeling better. Is this where all of your meetings take place? You never really told me what you did. Are you a paranormal psychic, maybe?" She had to ask for fun.

"No, but I do like the Sci-Fi Channel. Really, Janie, this is a favor I'm doing for a . . . friend."

As if satisfied with that answer, Janie pulled the side lever, pushing her seat back a bit, and stretched her long legs while placing her pale, manicured bare feet on the dash.

"Can't let my feet stay pasty white while the rest of my body fries. I really hate the idea of an inconsistent tan." With that, she smiled.

Taking his eyes off the wheel for a brief moment, Chase looked over to see her lean and toned body in a sexy flesh-colored sports bra and a pair of jeans. He would've loved to see a consistent tan and thought to mention the jeans should come off, but kept his mouth shut as she looked so beautifully peaceful soaking up the sun. He'd never met anyone so comfortable with themselves and carefree. Really, this had been a rough day and night in the desert, and she seemed completely at ease.

The drive was relaxing, and the soft bumps were somehow soothing. Janie drifted off and awoke as the Jeep stopped.

"We're here. You feel better? Your feet look great, by the way."

"Hmm." Looking down at her sun-kissed feet, Janie looked pleased with herself. "My legs will have to wait for the pool."

He pictured her lounging in a bikini by the pool, but had to put that thought aside for a minute. It was imperative this meeting went smoothly. He'd known Billy through his Chicago connections just enough to know he was dangerous—and extremely secretive. Chase needed someone who knew the casinos inside and out but would keep his mouth shut. He was investigating a certain casino for a major insurance company, Global Insurance. At the same time, Chase was tied in directly with a couple of high-powered casino bosses. Neither side knew of his association with the other, so Chase kept an unusually low profile. When he first met Janie and then again as he began to see her effect on him, he had wondered if she had some connection to the casino or if maybe the insurance company was checking up on him. Now, he just wanted to get to know more about her. He felt more protective of her as the day went by. He walked around to the passenger side to help Janie out of the Jeep. He noticed she had a tiny waist while lifting her to the ground. She gave him a sideways smirk.

She giggled, "What did I do to deserve this? I suppose the same applies here as most bars. No shirt, no shoes, no service."

"Maybe not here, but it'd be a good idea. I'd hate to have to rescue you from a leering cowboy or a deprived ghost."

She put her shirt on over her sports bra and felt his eyes watching her.

"Thank the Sun God for me that I didn't burn while sleeping. I cannot believe the heat here! Do you have a canopy or something for this Jeep?"

"Okay, enough about my car. I'll order you a great Bloody Mary, but you need to promise one thing."

"Sure, what is it?"

"Drink slowly and don't ask the bartender any questions. He takes things personally and doesn't have much of a sense of humor. Are we clear?"

"You got it."

They entered the bar through a half-round wooden door with a sign etched Pioneer Bar hanging askew. "Established 1898" was written in smaller font below. It looked like a refurbished shack that would have been in any John Wayne or Clint Eastwood movie. As Chase moved toward the bar with purpose, Janie walked slowly, taking in all of the old photos along the wall. She carefully ran her hand along the rough wood and wondered about the ghosts of the past. Most in the photos looked to be happy, though some somber. She wondered if they just didn't like to show their teeth back then. Chase was watching her while he waited for Blake, the bartender. Blake was also Billy's "assistant." Janie seemed really interested in one picture in particular as she leaned forward, narrowing her eyes to carefully inspect, and touched the glass as if it were an apparition.

Chase knew Billy did not like anyone touching the pictures, so he called, "Hey, Wounded One, I have your cure right here. Come on over and drink up!"

Janie jumped slightly and turned to look at Chase, feeling like she really had seen a ghost. As she walked over to the bar, she looked over her shoulder and peered once again at the photo of a group of men and a young woman in the middle of laughter with her head tilted back slightly, her arm around one man's neck, and her bobbed, wavy black hair covering one eye. The men looked at her adoringly as if they were there to amuse her. The man to her left, whom she had her arm around, seemed hopelessly in love. This looked to be the woman from her dream. She thought what a strange coincidence this was and felt a little light-headed.

Chapter 12

LOOKING PAST

"I think I need that drink about now." Janie flippantly added, "Who did you say owns this place?"

As if on cue, they were interrupted by Blake. He resembled the meanest, biggest steer wrestler in the West. In other words, not a good pick for a bar fight opponent. Surprisingly, he grinned at Chase and shook his hand as he placed a shot of whiskey in front of him.

He raised an eyebrow Janie's way in approval and asked, "Are you the little lady in need of one of my famous Bloody Marys? My friend here called ahead to warn me. Be careful, might put your tiny body over the edge." His laughter was deep and raucous as he reached over the bar to take her hand. "My name is Blake. When the crowd's in, they call me Bear. Sounds tougher. What do you think?"

"I think they're right. Fits the image, but I prefer Blake. Shows the real you, someone I'd like to know, I think."

"Chase, how do you find all the good ones? Should have nick-named you Lucky instead of Ace. By the way, Billy says everyone is more than happy at how things are going lately. He also left this for you." Blake handed over a manila envelope. "Says you may have quite a future here."

With that, Chase shot back the whiskey and watched in amusement how Janie managed to drink her Bloody Mary, making a pucker face after eating the vodka-soaked pickle. Blake's famous pickles are to the Bloody Mary what the worm is to an authentic bottle of tequila.

Janie suggested, "Wow, you should market these things. They pack quite a punch, Blake! I have high expectations for your cure. Much more than your Alka-Seltzer concoction, Chase." She looked at him sideways in amusement.

"She knows a professional when she sees one, Blake. On that note, I guess we'll head over to the casino and catch Billy later. I've got a meeting with O'Shea."

Blake nodded in approval, not only at the meeting with the head honcho of Hotel Du Monde, O'Shea, but also at Chase's choice of women, saying, "I think they are right. Your future is looking good."

As they were leaving, Janie couldn't help looking at the framed photographs on the way out. Just as if it were looking at her, she caught a glimpse of another photo of the same woman looking over her shoulder with her waves partially covering her face. She was in a white halter dress and blowing a kiss, like a dark version of Marilyn Monroe. She looked radiantly happy.

Without thinking, she asked a question she knew she shouldn't. "Blake, it was really nice meeting you. Who is the woman in this photo?"

Blake looked up at the picture, and Chase gave her a baffled stare. He shook his head slowly with a serious look in his eye. He knew Blake did not like questions from anyone in the business or associated with them.

Chase quickly grabbed her hand, saying, "Janie, I am really late. We can take a tour with the rest of the tourists another time." He practically yanked her to the Jeep, gave her a leg up into her seat, and they were off.

After they left, Blake took a long look at the picture of the beautiful and tragic past love of his boss, Billy Martinelli. As he stared at the photo, he noticed how uncanny the resemblance was to Janie, Chase's adorable catch.

As soon as they were on the road, Chase said, "What were you thinking, Janie? The one thing I told you not to do. He may seem nice, but underneath it all, Blake is a coldhearted guy who breaks up bar fights and other things for a living. He is very protective of the bar and its owner."

Janie felt confused and frustrated at the same time. She really wanted to find out about the woman in the photo who looked identical to the mother in her dream, but she did not want to anger Chase. "He seemed pretty easygoing to me. I'm sorry. It won't happen again."

She had been so preoccupied with sleeping and headaches that she hadn't taken much time to really look at Chase. She put on her sunglasses and pushed her seat back. Boy, did she get a good look at him now. He really was handsome in a rugged sort of way. To top it off, he had a sexy dimple on his right cheek when he smiled. She was a sucker for that.

Interrupting her thoughts, Chase said, "There she is. Vegas in her glory. Still hard to believe the first settlers to Sin City were Mormons. Even though some believe gambling to be a religion in its own right, I am sure that was not what William Bringhurst had in mind when he first settled here."

Janie was deep in thought as they drove up to the newest luxury hotel and casino, Du Monde, representing a plethora of cultures and countries from each continent. Each tile surrounding the main entrance represented one of the 193 different countries known to our world. It was truly beautiful and instantly popular with tourists. She was not just impressed but in awe of the concept. As they entered the lobby, Middle Eastern music was playing from an instrument with which she was unfamiliar. The chandeliers were all different styles and colors, yet they all felt cohesive. Janie thought it would be nice if that represented how we could all live together.

As Chase started walking to the front desk to check in, he held her wrist and stroked her pulse point with his thumb for the slightest moment. "You aren't taking off anywhere just yet, are you, Janie? I'd like to show you around."

"Uh, no," she said a little hesitantly. She smiled and waited for him to go up to the concierge. Her smile faded as soon as his back turned.

In a strange panic, Janie felt out of breath. She needed air and quickly. After taking a few different turns, she spied the colorful pool outside. Immediately, she threw open the door and went to the first cabana in view. There were only a few people at the pool as it was late afternoon, and most were heading in to get ready for the evening. She quickly took off her clothes, except for her matching nude sports bra and string bikini underwear. She dove into the inviting, cool water and swam until she felt herself calming down and her breathing returning to normal. Somewhere in her mind, she knew she had nowhere to go and not a soul to call on. Yet, Janie was as sure as the hot Vegas day was long that she needed to be here to uncover the meaning of her haunting dreams. She needed to know more about the woman in those photos.

As she finished a lap and grabbed the edge of the pool, she looked up into Chase's amused face. "Do you christen every hotel pool this way? Can I offer you a cozy robe and a proposition?"

Chapter 13

A FAVOR CALLED IN

L ooking into his eyes, Janie carefully replied to the idea of a proposition, saying, "I'll take that robe for sure, and listen to what you have to say. I don't know what came over me, Chase, but it felt great to take a swim. Looks kind of like a suit anyway, doesn't it?"

Chase looked her up and down longingly, and resisted putting the robe around her. "Nice try. Hey, do you have plans for the night yet? Did you get in touch with your people already?"

Janie furrowed her brow and looked down for a long moment. When she looked up, he could read the sadness and confusion in her eyes. Softly, Janie whispered, "I . . . I don't know who I'd call at the moment." Then, as if she was not allowed those emotions, she said with a smile, "Besides, I haven't had a tour."

"I'd like to give you more than a tour if you'll accept my invitation. I could really use your help tonight with a dilemma in the casino. I promise I'll be a perfect gentleman. Will you stay here tonight?"

Without any awkward hesitation, she answered "yes."

He loved her direct attitude and quiet confidence. He said he promised her a tour after she got dressed. Chase indirectly worked with this hotel and couldn't really have his friend run around a five-star resort in a robe. He handed her a key. "I've got a meeting. It should last only a couple of hours. I'll have some necessities and things sent up for you in the next thirty minutes, okay?"

"I'm looking forward to a hot shower. I'll see you later." She left him with a wide smile.

Chase knew exactly what to do prior to his meeting. Janie was not only strikingly beautiful, but totally unlike any woman he'd ever met. She made no demands, did not seem intimidated, and was perfectly at ease in any situation. Yet, she really gave away very little about herself. The look she gave him earlier at the pool was his only indication that she had her own share of secrets. He wondered what or who she might be hiding from. In the meantime, he got a good enough glimpse of her body to figure out her size and surprise her with a few things from Chez Mathilde. He knew the manager and was sure she'd send up something perfect for Janie to wear this evening.

Upon entering room 3372, Janie saw that this was no ordinary hotel room. It was a spectacular suite with a French motif. The chandeliers were beautiful and delicate, with a mix of antique gold, crystals, and amber and tourmaline stones. The floors were two warm colors of marble squares set at an angle, with lovely ornate rugs and beautiful furniture. She was sure each room depicted a different country or element of mixed cultures. The bathroom was exquisite. With a claw-foot tub and a huge shower, its floor and tile were mosaic while the fixtures were antique gold. She stepped out of her robe and underwear into the steam shower. Just as the pool felt refreshing and numbed her senses a bit, the hot, steamy shower allowed Janie to relax totally in peace and quiet while letting down her protective layer. She closed her eyes and let the water envelop her body. After a few minutes, she realized she was sobbing uncontrollably, which felt like a much-needed release. Finally, she collected herself and took several deep breaths, taking in the eucalyptus-lavender aromatherapy within the steam shower. She felt as if a weight had been lifted and was ready to have a nice evening. Unsure of Chase's "proposition," Janie put that thought aside as her stomach growled.

There was a knock at the door. She threw on the soft robe and cushy thong slippers and opened the door without a worry as to who it might be. The young bellhop eyed her with a polite yet approving smile and presented a cloth bag full of clothes. He also handed Janie a card and set up a vase of flowers, laid down a tray of cheese, fruit, and crackers, and poured a glass of Champagne.

As he left, he looked at Janie very sweetly and said, "Miss, he's a lucky man. Have a nice evening."

Janie thought him so sweet and felt terrible that she hadn't any cash to give him a tip. She did not know what to say but simply walked up to him, brushed his cheek with a kiss, and quietly told him, "Thank you."

The young man was embarrassed and thrilled with his "payment" and thought her to be gracious and beautiful. He hoped he'd have an opportunity to see Mr. Chase O'Leary with her later to see how this story unfolded. The other women he'd seen Chase with were nothing like her—and never in his room.

Starved, Janie ravaged the fruit and cheese platter. The champagne was perfect after her relaxing shower. The robe was so comfortable that she barely thought to look in the bag. As she pulled out the items one by one, her jaw dropped at his sense of detail. He had thought of everything. There was a beautiful strapless mini dress of blush chiffon and nude sequins placed sporadically throughout. It was stunning. The strappy silvery, gold high heels were expensive and sexy. He had even included a pearl-and-diamond choker necklace. On top of all this, Chase thought of the lacy La Perla underwear and strapless bra. She thought he must be a pretty damn good judge of women as his sizing and taste were perfect. The dress fit like a sophisticated glove, and the shoes made her long legs look even longer. She was only slightly embarrassed that he picked her 34B bra size correctly. As she opened the card, she noticed it smelled like lilac.

Dear Janie,

> *Please meet me in the Bar Terra Nova at 8. I hope you like my taste in clothes. Only you can do that dress justice. Thanks for sticking around.*

—Chase

> *P.S. If the clothes do not fit or are not your style, please call down to Chez Mathilde in the hotel. Talk to Mirabel.*

Janie looked satisfied at her reflection in the mirror. It felt great to blow-dry her wavy hair smooth. She took out the minimal makeup she had in her purse and applied the eyeliner, mascara, and lip gloss. Thanks to the drive through the desert, she had great color. On her way downstairs to meet Chase, she truly wondered about his motivations for the evening. She wondered about where he grew up and what piqued his interest in her.

Chapter 14

CHASING ACE

From the outside looking in, Chase O'Leary seemed to have a charmed life. He had been a beautiful child who became an even better-looking young man. His father was a police officer, always there to keep him from trouble. His mother brought her prize-winning pies to the neighbors if he accidentally threw a ball through their window or lit a tree on fire with a bottle rocket. It seemed he was always in on the action and a magnet for girls as well as leader to the boys. He had charisma to the *n*th degree and charming good looks to go along with it—a dangerous combination.

From an early age, he was extremely intuitive, reading people quickly. Quick enough that it took him only one fat lip to understand that when his father drank, he'd better stay out of his way. His mother knew only too well from experience and always had dinner on the table by six sharp. The house was also kept impeccably clean. Chase noticed that the fights ending with his dad raising a hand to his mom usually involved money. As soon as he was able, he worked by collecting bottles and cans and doing odd jobs so he wouldn't have to ask his mother or father for a dime.

Everyone took a liking to Chase, even the local bookies who hung out at the pool hall. He wasn't supposed to go in there, but his best friend's uncle owned the place and let them in to learn a few "life lessons," as he called it. By twelve, he and Johnny could beat some of the regulars at a game of pool. Of course, no money was allowed to change hands.

Johnny's Uncle Mac would say, "You both won fair and square, and you entertained these fellas with your tenacity. Go to Danny's Groceries and pick up my carton of smokes he owes me. If you're both back here in ten minutes, I'll give you two dollars each. I'll be timing you. *Go!*"

They heard Mac and the guys laugh as they left, but they raced and laughed all the way there and back, never knowing the true nature of these so-called errands.

Just as he was learning about pool, Chase's father started taking him to his Thursday night poker games to ensure his son did not grow up a mama's boy. Chase watched carefully and was able to discern instinctively who was bluffing. He read body language perfectly.

One Thursday before the big poker game, he mentioned to his dad, "Hey, you know every time Jimmy rubs his thumbnail, he's hiding something. Also, Tony squints his eyes and slightly raises his left eyebrow when he has a really good hand."

His dad said, "What the hell are you talking about, kid? How could you see all that in just a month of coming with me? I've been playing with these guys for years. Go on and get your hat and quit makin' things up. You know what I think of liars."

That evening, Joe couldn't help but take note of what his son had said. He watched Jimmy and Tony carefully. Sure enough, Jimmy played with his thumb and had not a prayer with his cards, and Tony's left eyebrow arched before he upped the ante to call everyone out and win the hand with a full house of aces over kings. He decided to keep the information to himself and win some money off these jokers for once.

Later that night, on the way home, he whispered to Chase, "I have a new name for you, son. In my work, one earns his nickname. I think 'Ace' is appropriate."

This made Chase smile a broad, crooked smile, making his dimple pop. He had never been so proud of himself as tonight. It was the first time his father showed him respect. The nickname stuck. Before long, all Mac's guys, the Southside police beat, and his own friends called him Ace. It suited him well.

Knowing how the force worked and watching Chase all these years, Mac was sure Chase could make his own life easier and help Mac's business run more smoothly, if it weren't for his father getting in the way. Aside from his drinking, Joe was straight as an arrow. Mac had to find a way to gain Chase's confidence and turn him against his dad.

He decided to tell him about the time his mother had turned to his wife, Mary, after her husband, Joe, had beaten her nearly to death. She didn't want anyone, especially her son, to know.

She winced in pain from the iodine as she whimpered in a quivering voice, "Tell everyone I had to go to Wisconsin to see my sick aunt." She stayed with Mary for ten days only to return to the drunken bastard belittling her on a daily basis.

Mac let Chase know what a sought-after woman she had been before and what a damn shame it was she ended up with Joe. "I'm sorry to say this to you, Ace, but I care about you and your mother. I want you to be able to take care of yourselves if your father goes on a bender. You might want to have a little savings of your own if you need it, you know what I'm saying?"

"Yes, Mac, I hear ya." From then on, Chase began hanging out more often with Mac and the boys.

Hanging around the pool hall was the most exciting time of Chase's life. While everyone else seemed a bit depressed about the economic downturn, this was not the case at Mac's place. All were met with a big thumbs-up and a chummy smack on the back as soon as they walked in. Sixteen never felt so good. Chase was ecstatic to get a "promotion" and be paid by Mac's Boys. Now, the errands he ran became a real job. Even though Chase kept most of his money hidden away so it looked as if he made the same amount as the other kids his age, his father grew suspicious of Mac. A police officer, after all, Joe knew Mac was shady. If Chase continued hanging around Mac and his crowd, he was going to end up in big trouble down the road.

As time went on, everyone had a lot of faith in Chase. Not only did they see him win over the women, but he had a trustworthy face and wit about him. The cops liked his respectful attitude, as did the other shop owners. Mac gave him more and more responsibility. With that responsibility, he was more likely to find trouble with the law. He was not yet in a "right-hand man" position, which would buy him out of most troubles. Therefore, if he were caught, the consequences would need to be paid. Jail was inevitable.

Chase had finished making the rounds and collecting from the local businesses when a new, younger kid approached him looking scared. Chase grabbed both his shoulders and looked him square in the eyes, saying, "Jesus, Marky, you look like you're going to piss your pants. Get it together. Give me that package. I'll take care of it today." He was caught off guard.

Chapter 15

TAKING THE HIT

Marky handed him the package of drugs and ran. Within minutes, two policemen new to this beat walked alongside Chase. Assuming they were all down with the game, Chase smiled at them both with a flippant "Afternoon, gentlemen."

Marky had squealed for sure, and they grabbed both his arms and the package. He was placed under arrest immediately upon uncovering its contents. Chase was given some leniency by the judge, but still sentenced to one year in prison. With good behavior, his attorney assured him it would be no more than six months. Within that time, he was fully expected to keep his mouth shut. This, of course, went without saying.

Chase handled prison fine, but was approached a couple of times by the DEA wanting to give him a quick out in return for more information. He simply stuck to the story that he found the package on the ground, which they knew was untrue. Marky only knew Chase as his point of contact and nothing more. It was enough of a testimony to land him where he was for a while. Other than the occasional harassment from the DEA, he was treated well by both the inmates and the guards. Word got around that he was not to be messed with. He was given special privileges with female visitors and certain foods for his "allergies."

The toughest day in prison was finding out his father had died knowing what his kid had become. He did not visit Chase other than the first week when he was trying to get him to fess up and give him information. His mother was heartbroken but never failed to visit weekly with his favorite homemade banana bread and letting him know she was praying for him every day and attending Mass twice a week now.

"You promise me, honey, that you will go to confession," she would say. "I know Father Daniel comes here on a regular basis."

After his father died, Chase had a heavy heart. He knew working for Mac was not a good or smart way to live, but it got him through some hard times and taught him a lot. These guys had become more of a family to him than his own. Somehow, he would figure out a way to make a respectable living and get his mother away from Chicago, yet avoid offending his other family. He'd need to get creative.

The day he was released outside of the prison walls, Chase had mixed emotions. He was elated to be free but a little nervous to see Mac and the boys. He knew how careful he had been by disclosing nothing, but they still let him out pretty early. He assumed it was due to his father's influence and death. Maybe it was the least his fellow officers could do for him. Because of this early release, Chase hoped none of the guys were suspicious that he may have talked. He knew only too well what happened to snitches.

As he entered the pool hall, everyone gave him quiet nods and shook his hand. Mac and Johnny, his best friend, were missing, which raised a flag for Chase. He was greeted with a pat on the back by Mac's right-hand watchdog, Tony. Tony did a lot of the dirty work for Mac. Now, Chase was beginning to get more than a little panicked. He smiled outwardly as he continued to wipe his sweaty palms on his worn jeans. Tony asked him to take a walk and debrief, so to speak.

Chapter 16

RECKONING

As they walked, Tony put his arm on Chase's shoulder, squeezing his muscle a little too tightly, saying, "I just want to get the low-down on anything you may have heard while in the pen, Ace."

Chase held his ground and worked on keeping his breathing easy. "Uh, sure, Tony. Because of your help on the outside, it wasn't so bad inside. Thanks for making my stay at the Grand Hotel far more pleasant than it could have been," he uttered with a slight laugh, trying to sound cool and not nervous.

As they walked a few blocks and turned in the direction of the old warehouse building, Chase thought of running but knew he had no chance at that time. These guys didn't have a problem with shooting you in the back.

He managed to keep up his air of confidence even as Tony said, "I want to show you some new merchandise in the warehouse and see what you think."

"Sure thing, Tony. How's business been while I've been gone, anyway?"

"Well, here we are, Ace. You first."

Chase pulled hard on the heavy steel door and heard a loud blast. For a moment, he thought he was dead or shot. The terrified expression on his face said it all. The place was filled with people and laughter. They had arranged a party for Chase's return and knew just what they were doing with this surprise. Mac and Johnny came up and slapped him on the back and hugged him all the while cracking up in fits of laughter.

Johnny could barely get the words out through his gasps: "You should have seen your face, man! You looked like you had met your Maker. I thought you were going to fall over right there! Thank God you didn't. Did you see the women waiting for you? Didn't know you were such a ladies' man. They all couldn't wait for you to get out."

"You asshole, Johnny! I will get you back for this!" He could finally relax and laugh while saying it.

Mac came up to him next and quietly spoke into Chase's ear: "Ace, you have done me proud, kid." He handed him a very thick packet without saying anything further.

After a couple weeks things settled down a bit. Chase decided to approach Mac with his plans.

"Mac, you have been like a father to me. I know you've been giving me choice jobs and more responsibility. I need to take my mom somewhere away from here and regroup. I've thought about ways I can help you, her, and myself all at the same time. I want to go to Las Vegas. I can stay below the radar and learn the law so that I can always be one step ahead. I would also like to understand how these casinos are run. I know you have some contacts in this area. Of course, I won't become an attorney any time soon with my record, but I may learn enough to evade the law. Prison, while made much better for me by you, was still no picnic. I'd like to stay away from that place. What do you think?"

Although Mac was disappointed, he began to see the potential of having another smart and talented ally on the legal side of things to help out when he was really in a bind. He also knew there was a ton of money to be had in Vegas, and he would be interested in getting a piece of the action and inside information from someone he trusted.

"I always knew you were special, Ace. Even your name will suit you well in Vegas. I'll see what I can do to get you started on your way next week. I've got a friend, Billy, who may be able to get you into some poker games for good money. You're one of the best here. Besides, that packet I gave you ought to give you and your mother a jump start."

Chase and Mac talked a while longer, and he felt like the world was his to explore. Without his father looking over his shoulder, he moved to Vegas with his mother and set her up nicely. In fact, one of her high school friends lived nearby and showed her all around.

Now he was free to piece it all together. Like most things, this too came easily to Chase. Within a year, he was making money hand over fist in high-stake poker games and taking classes on criminal justice at a community college. While in the casinos, Chase paid close attention to security and how everything worked. Billy helped him talk to the right people and eventually Chase was known as Ace, the expert at poker and finding cracks in security. Soon, the contacts and money began to pour in.

All of it perfectly legal.

Chapter 17

A PUZZLE OF PIECES

There is nothing like a beautiful dress and diamonds to make a woman feel like a million bucks. Janie swept her silky hair up, showing her swan-like neck, slipped on the strapless dress and high-heeled shoes, and carefully clasped the delicate diamond-and-pearl choker. She felt as if she were walking on a catwalk in a fashion show rather than down the hallway of the Hotel Du Monde. She knew Chase would be waiting for her. For the first time since they'd met, Janie had butterflies. This seemed real now, like an actual date.

In the elevator, two men heading to the casino eyed her longingly and exchanged looks. She knew she looked dressed to kill, but hoped Chase would think so too. As she walked through the lobby, Janie did not notice the admiring stares. With undaunting grace, she sauntered to the bar where Chase had chosen to meet. She wondered what he had up his sleeve. He had asked her to help him out with something this evening and that probably had a lot to do with the outfit. In retrospect, he seemed to be fairly protective of her, so she hoped he didn't expect anything that would put her in a compromising situation.

At first, she didn't see him standing at the corner high-top table, but Chase definitely saw her, as did the rest of the well-dressed men in the bar. She looked more sophisticated and beautiful than he imagined in that dress with her hair piled sexily on her head.

He walked up to her and their eyes met. "You look incredible, and the dress fits you beautifully. I am honored to buy you a drink, Miss Blue."

Dressed as he was in a tux, he took her breath away. So far, she had only seen him in jeans, unshaven, and with messy hair. Wow! He was straight out of *GQ* tonight. His blondish-brown hair was on the longish side, but tonight it looked shorter and cleaner with lighter blond streaks from the sun running through it. His piercing gray eyes made her feel like he could see right through her. Chase had a great tan, which, set against the white, crisp shirt, looked amazing.

"Well, no longer are you a sight for sore eyes. I'll happily accept that cocktail." She had to add with the excitement of a little girl, "Chase, you're the best. I love the ensemble and had a great time getting ready, thanks to you! I thought you had an eye for detail, but had no idea you could read my mind."

Chase thought he'd like to read more than her mind as he ordered a dirty martini for himself and a lemontini for Janie. He was about to ask her what she wanted to do in Las Vegas when she interrupted him with her usual straightforward attitude.

"So, cutting to the chase, no pun intended, what favor do you need from me?"

"Let's have a drink first and relax. I'm not sure just yet how you can help, but I know I like you standing across from me right now. It is touchy information I'm trying to obtain from someone, and I am not sure you are the right person for this, Janie. I don't want to get you in an uncomfortable situation as I don't know this guy very well."

"What do you mean? Who is this guy, and exactly what are you expecting?" she said, a little bit offended.

"Nothing like I think you're thinking. I just need to find out if the casino management is friends with the tall, dark-haired gentleman in the opposite corner behind you—don't look now—and what business he has at this casino. I thought maybe you and I could gamble and . . ."

Janie cut him off midsentence and raised her voice so all could hear: "Just what kind of a girl do you think I am? I should have known your type from the moment you drove up!" As if completely outraged, she added insult to injury by throwing the remainder of her lemontini at him, just missing his face.

Chase didn't know what to think as she stormed off to the other side of the bar. He did not know this would upset her so much; however, it was a touchy favor. He had been about to tell her that they could gamble a while and perhaps he could entice the mystery man who held the key as to whether or not this casino was going to make some very illegal moves into playing a high-stakes game of poker. At the same time, they could work on gathering invaluable information. This gathering of information did not entail Janie spending any quality time with the guy alone. He liked her too much already for that. Now, he didn't think he knew her well enough to understand if he had pissed her off just enough to do something erratic, like when she jumped in the swimming pool in her underwear. On the other hand, if she really knew how to get the guy to talk, perhaps she was playing a very convincing game. Either way, he'd find out more about him and watch them from afar if something went awry.

Chapter 18

MR. WRONG

Chase watched the man approach Janie almost immediately and offer to buy her a drink. He looked over at Chase with shrugged shoulders, a thin, sarcastic mouth, and a raised eyebrow as if to say, "Too bad, buddy, you blew it." After that, he raised a finger to the bartender, ordering a new drink for Janie, and put his palm on her supple, bare back. Chase was definitely jealous. However, he had put himself—and her—in this position. He decided to ask around and find out about Mr. Wrong.

"My name is Clay Dixon. I saw you the minute you walked in the bar and hate to admit that I was ecstatic when you looked 'free' from your date. You are too beautiful to be upset. I believe you had a sour martini, but I've ordered you some champagne to match your beautiful dress and celebrate our chance meeting."

"Charmed, I'm sure, Clay. I'm Janie Blue. I am still a little upset and glad you came to my side so that Chase would not."

Janie was sure by mentioning Chase, Clay would bite and start asking questions to which Janie would filter her answers carefully.

She was surprised at how naturally this cat-and-mouse game felt. First, Clay glanced in the corner of the bar to see if Chase was looking and then looked relieved that he was gone. Janie had no fear at the moment, but hoped Chase didn't think she was too upset with him. She had to make him believe she had been truly offended or certainly he would've followed her to the bar, letting go of his real reason for being there in the first place.

"So, Miss Blue, what is your relation to Chase? He seemed to really infuriate you."

With a haughty, nonchalant attitude, she responded, "He is a charming guy I met a couple of days ago. He asked too many questions. Most of which I really did not want to answer. I am certain he put his own spin on my life with one too many unattractive assumptions. That is all she wrote, my friend. Can we talk about how much fun there is to be had in Las Vegas?"

Clay could only imagine where this exquisite creature came from, but he did not care. He wanted her and planned to show her a fantastic time tonight—all night.

"I am not sure where you are from, but I detect a Southern accent. I do not want to assume or ask too many questions, so I'll just say, I am going to gamble and would love for you to join me."

"I'd enjoy learning whatever you can teach me, Clay. I am quite the novice. What's your favorite game?"

Clay had a great answer but decided on saying, "Blackjack and craps. More luck with craps, and it attracts quite a crowd when you win. Blackjack is more of an art."

"Then, blackjack it is. I'd like to think that in both gambling and life, it takes more than just luck to win."

As they sat at the blackjack table for a hundred dollars a hand, Clay looked at Janie playfully and asked, "So, Janie, what special talents do you have?"

She wanted to tell him she had a photographic memory and wasn't bad at counting cards, but instead just smiled mischievously, saying,

"You'll just have to wait and see what tricks I have up my sleeve."

"Except, you're not wearing any sleeves this evening, my dear. Shall I look elsewhere?"

"Very coy of you. Shall we begin the lesson? I am an eager student."

Janie hadn't seen or heard anything unusual yet and wondered how long she'd have to play this game of wit with Clay before she gained any information worth talking about to Chase. He was actually pretty decent company if it weren't for the constant sexual innuendos. She decided to have another drink, as the waitresses asked about every five minutes. After drinking her second glass of champagne, Janie felt a little light-headed and thought about holding off on ordering any more. Truth be told, she felt a bit uneasy around Clay, and the cocktails made her relax. *Why not?* she thought. *Three is my limit tonight.*

As her third glass came with a cute, blue umbrella to match the drink he ordered for her, Janie was having a great time. Just when she was about to win another hand, a stately, gray-haired man walked up to Clay and told him that O'Shea, the Du Monde casino boss, wanted a word with him later.

The stern-looking gentleman patted Clay on the back, saying, "You will be perfect for the part." At his departure, he winked in a sophisticated way and eyed Janie as if wondering where he had seen her before.

Chapter 19

ROSE-COLORED GLASSES

Janie's eyes were a little blurry and she was a tiny bit dizzy. In her tipsy confidence, she asked, "Will you be starring in a play soon, Clay?"

"What are you talking about, pretty little miss? Looks like you're winning. I didn't need to teach you at all. In fact, I'd say you're a little too good," he murmured the last part.

As she kept her eyes on the cards and motioned to the dealer to hold, she said, "I overheard that guy say you'd be perfect for the part. Are you an up-and-coming movie star or is there a new show in Vegas?"

"FYI, that was not just anyone, but a higher-up at the casino. Seems they think I am talented and may need my assistance sometime soon."

He wanted to impress her, so he went on to say they gave him a lot of extra privileges here that he could show her later this evening in his room. He couldn't help noticing that she continued to win consistently and whispered, "Janie, better stop now or I may lose my job."

Clay wanted to get her to his room sooner than later and ordered her another drink.

"Hey, don't forget I'd like a green umbrella this time!" she said with a laugh a bit louder and longer than normal. She definitely was in over her head.

Not far away but hidden from their sight, Chase watched in both amusement and envy. He laughed to himself about Janie's low tolerance for cocktails, but grew more concerned that it would seriously cloud her judgment with Clay Dixon. He was waiting on some information from Blake, the bartender at the Pioneer Saloon and Billy's best informant. It looked like they might be there a while. Chase left to have a chat with Jerry, the matchmaker of the casino for high rollers. He had instant connections with the most beautiful and high-class women around. Chase knew right where to find him—at the smoky cigar bar. It was the only bar with smoking privileges in the hotel, which made it pretty popular.

"Hey, Jerry, it's been a while. You're looking satisfied as usual."

"My main man, Ace. Never a complaint from the ladies. In fact, they all line up for you. What can I do for you?"

"I'll text you with a room number. I need two of the more creative and adventurous girls ready to go for this evening. They will be seeing Clay Dixon ASAP, okay? I owe you one."

"Don't worry, Ace. I know where to find you. And, I know his type."

With that, Chase went back to check on Janie and Clay. On his way back, Blake called about Clay.

"Chase, you know he's connected with O'Shea, right? Also, he's a badass with the ladies from what I hear around the bar."

"Okay, I wasn't sure about either of those two comments. Is there an upcoming project he is on? What do you mean by 'badass'? Do they all dig him or does he push them around?"

"Man, Ace, you have a lot of questions. Two of which I can answer you on the phone. You have a meeting tomorrow morning with O'Shea and Dixon of which I was going to page you just before you rang. Secondly, he is more than rough and takes no accountability, especially if there are no strings and connections with the women. Why are you asking?"

Chapter 20

IN AN INSTANT

I n a slight panic as he felt he had taken his eye off Janie for too long, Chase curtly responded, "Thanks for the info, Blake. I'm now in a huge rush."

"Wait a minute, Chase. You still with that little hottie you brought in? If so, Billy wants you to bring her to the meeting with him on Sunrise Street tomorrow evening."

"What? Why?" But instead of waiting for an answer, he said, "Later, Blake."

Out of breath, he did not see Janie or Clay anywhere on the casino floor. This probably meant they had gone to his room. Chase had to find that number and knew only one person to ask. Jaxon, liaison to the casino owner, O'Shea. He had dirt on everyone within the casino. Chase dialed his number.

"Hey Jax, you on the casino floor right now? It's Chase. I need some information quickly."

"If it's not the one and only Ace. What can I do for you tonight?"

"I'm surprising Clay Dixon with some girls from Jerry so as to make sure he's relaxed and happy for our meeting in the morning. I need his room number."

"Well, I know about tomorrow and can give you the info you need, but I'll have you know I saw him with a smoking-hot number in the casino. In fact, I thought I noticed you with her earlier," he said rather smugly. "She looks like someone I knew a long time ago. That is a face you don't forget. He's in the West Penthouse. I don't want any problems before tomorrow, okay?"

"No problems, Jax. Thanks. I'll touch base with you later."

Immediately, he called Jerry with the penthouse suite, saying, "I hope they are ready to head up right now."

"Absolutely, in the lobby by the west elevator. I'll page them now. See you around, Ace."

Chase thanked him, hung up the phone, and almost sprinted to the extra set of elevators in the back reserved for personnel only. He used his card to call the elevator and hit WP; it took him directly to the West Penthouse lobby. Although he was not quite ready for this scene, he was relieved to see they hadn't made it into the bedroom as of yet. Dixon had Janie pinned against the rough, grass-cloth wallpaper with his right knee positioned between her legs and his mouth hard on her lips. He held her head with one hand and roughly gripped a hunk of her long hair with the other while she struggled. Chase could not make out what he was saying, but it sounded like he'd lost patience with toying with his prey and was about to pounce. Chase had to hold back his anger and treat this situation very politically and quickly.

With a more than slight "Uhmm," he continued, "Excuse me, you two. Dixon, I've got some important information for you." Clay jerked his head toward Chase.

He handed Clay a note letting him know of the two very adventurous and anxious ladies arriving at his suite any minute. He looked at Chase with daggers in his eyes, yet he was also intrigued and slightly amused at the note he read.

Chase said quietly to Janie, with a look clearly asking her to trust him on this one, "We have to finish our earlier conversation before you leave tomorrow."

Just in time, two beautiful, scantily dressed women were giggling and knocking on the penthouse door.

Clay called down the hall, "Ladies, wait just a moment. I believe you are looking for me. As for you, Janie, if your talk does not go well, I will find you tomorrow. And, Chase, as you so interrupted me with this surprise and annoyance, I will forgive this as we may be working together in the near future. I *will* see you in the morning."

"Nice evening to you, Clay," Chase said with a smile through gritted teeth.

Without saying a word, he gently took Janie's arm and pulled her shaken body toward him as he led her into the elevator.

Chapter 21

IN GOOD TIME

The rest of the world might follow all of the rules. Ella's father, however, was not about to sit around and find out about his daughter's body found in some lake in a back-ass-ward town, murdered by a fanatical serial killer on the way to her aunt's house. Mike refused to wait seventy-two hours for the police to take a half-witted look around for her. He had some connections from living on the island off Seattle for twenty-five years now and knew the locals well. He'd gone to every police fundraiser as well as any local fundraiser period since he could remember. He would work those contacts and owed favors without hesitation if he didn't get through to her husband.

"Listen, Dan," Mike said, raising his voice. "I know you are worried too, but I don't know why Ella would take this long getting to her aunt's without calling one of us, do you?"

Dan calmly replied, "I know when there is a death in the family, people do funny things and need more time to reflect. I should've gone with her and did not. I think she was pretty pissed about that too. Maybe she is just taking some time. I have people looking, Mike. Hard. Just give me twenty-four hours. I'd hate to cause an unnecessary reason to give the press free rein to go crazy all because Ella needed some peace and quiet for a couple of days. We've checked with the hospitals, so we know she is not there. We've also checked accidents and auto-theft reports. For all we know, she's at a hotel doing yoga and getting massages until she decides to face reality or feels she's mourned enough alone for her mother."

Still very fresh and heavy on his heart, Mike lowered his head in mention of his wife's death and quietly said, "She did act a little funny just before leaving, and I did spring her mom's car on her at the last minute. Perhaps you are right. Still, twenty-four hours, okay? Then we get the police involved."

Dan was relieved. He had checked more places than he mentioned and definitely had his best and most secretive guy on this. Marco was a true professional in every sense. The last thing Dan needed during this campaign was the press focusing on Ella having a breakdown. Or maybe she knew more about his sordid affair with Melanie than she let on. He would find out one way or the other. But he just didn't believe she was in danger at the moment. Clearly, he was mostly concerned about his career.

On Mike's way back home, he reminisced about how he and his wife had come to "adopt" Janie and call her Ella when she was not yet five years old. They swore to ensure that only a rare few knew she wasn't their biological child. He knew the world could be a pretty lonely, frightening place at that age, especially since she could not even remember her name let alone anything about her past. At the same time, Janie did not know how lucky she was that money and power could pass her situation through 99.9 percent of the red tape involved in foster care or adoption. This allowed her to begin a new life without ever knowing the tragedy that had caused her post-traumatic stress disorder and amnesia.

During the three months in which she did not speak, there was a lot going on. There were numerous interviews between the Rosses' attorney and various counselors and doctors before a conclusion was reached: living with the Rosses and becoming a permanent member of their household was best for Janie. They all worked out that unless Janie brought up the past, she would now be known strictly as Ella Ross. The Rosses decided to begin an altogether new life in Washington as legal parents of Ella.

Ella adapted well to her new life with few questions. This pleasantly surprised them. For the three months she stayed in the Rosses' doctor's care, she was subliminally shown pictures of Kate and Mike Ross and their parents, representing them as her family. She was told her name was Ella over and over while being subjected to scenes of a happy home where everyone smiled. Thinking this was the logical path to take, they were re-creating Janie/Ella's memories. In other situations, Mike knew, this could be thought of as brainwashing.

Finally, after three months, Mike and Kate picked Ella up. She smiled shyly but still said nothing. The doctor was certain she would speak soon once in her new environment, which was familiar to her through all of the pictures and videos. With the latest technology of the time, they were even able to add Ella in here and there. They had found Lizzie's pictures and photo albums, so they could have them around when Ella asked what she looked like as a baby. Of course, they removed any that may trigger a bad memory or any emotion at all. They simply wanted to obliterate her past and hoped she would never remember. This was her life now as it had always been.

After a bit Janie/Ella seemed happy. She was laughing and talking and all the while fully believing in her role as Ella Ross, Kate and Mike's daughter. They spoiled her rotten with the frilliest clothes, ballet lessons, tiaras, stuffed animals, and a room that looked like it came straight out of a fairy tale. She did not have pets.

One day, she saw a little white poodle puppy in the pet store window. Mike remembered her standing frozen, mesmerized by the tiny animal. Kate and Mike both held their breath, wondering if Ella would remember the horrible scene where her puppy lay mangled in front of her, not far from her dying mother.

In an instant, Ella seemed to take a breath. She blinked her eyes a couple of times and told them in a low voice, "Mommy and Daddy, I don't think I ever want a puppy. I think they just get in the way."

They did not know what to say. Mike saw Kate fight back tears, and he said, "You know, honey, Mommy is allergic to dogs and cats, so we cannot have one, remember?"

Ella responded in the typical way of a five-year-old: "I forgot about your bless-yous when we were at the park."

That was that. Potential flood of memories rushing back avoided. The only other time Ella seemed to have a really bad day was after Kate took her to see a Dr. Seuss kind of children's play entitled *Why Ask Why?* Late in the evening, she came into their room screaming about a nightmare in which she kept seeing the letter *Y* with blood dripping all around. It seemed very disturbing to her, and neither of them knew why that would trigger anything strange, so they decided to drop it unless Ella had more nightmares.

The PTSD amnesia she experienced as a young child made Mike worry that maybe Ella's mother's death had triggered something. He could not tell Dan yet as no one else except her doctor and his parents (who had since died) knew she was adopted. He hoped Dan found out some positive answers soon. After all, he had better connections in the political world than Mike had in his world of finance. He would try to maintain his composure until he heard back from Dan. At home, he opened the door to the large, empty home, ran his fingers through his thinning brown hair with hints of gray, and felt completely alone.

At two in the morning, Dan's private cell phone rang. This one was rogue, and only Marco, his more than secret associate who saved his ass on a daily basis, had this number. This probably meant only one thing.

Chapter 22

HOT ON THE TRAIL

"**D**id you find her?"

"We found her car, Dan. It was abandoned at a mechanic's shop outside of Vegas. Luckily, the shop's owner ran out of steam and came back early from a fishing trip. He saw the car in bad shape parked behind his shop. Any idea why she would've been heading in that direction? It looked pretty beat up—like she'd been in an accident."

"Shit! Find her, Marco! Check your Vegas contacts. Show her picture, but tell them to be very discreet."

"Already on it, Dan. One of my contacts believes they may have a location on her. Strange thing is, they are pretty sure they saw her check into a hotel in Las Vegas with a man. I'm waiting for definite confirmation, but probably won't get it until tomorrow around nine or ten, okay?"

"That little slut," Dan muttered as he hung up the phone.

He then rolled over in bed and put his lean arm over Melanie, his mistress, who was sound asleep lying next to him. His ego and narcissistic nature were definitely going to destroy him politically if he couldn't learn to control his urges. He had to take a sleeping pill to try and drift off again.

He thought, "This cannot be happening right now. That bitch had better not ruin my career."

Dan wondered why the fact that she could be with someone else infuriated him so badly since he had had other women on more occasions than he could count during their marriage. It was not that he didn't find his wife attractive. She was so goddamn beautiful and sweet, and everyone held her in such high esteem that he never felt good enough for her. However, he would never bring himself to admit his self-indulgence and narcissism. As if to add more credibility to his intimidation of Ella, she was a little too cautious. The women he went after were less educated, slightly pretty, insecure, and saw him as a god. He just decided to blame Ella and hold a grudge against her. The thing was, he could not leave her, as she was the perfect politician's wife. He could not have paid an actress to play the part better.

He thought he needed to get to the bottom of this. If she truly was having an outright affair, she may be better off having an "accident."

At 3 a.m., Marco hadn't had any Ella sightings and decided to get some rest. He would find out who the two different men were in the photos and their association to Ella. He knew this was not going to end well. He never pegged Ella for having an affair, but she must be having some sort of crisis approaching thirty or quite possibly deliberately trying to sabotage her husband's career because of his piggish behavior. He had little respect for Dan's personal life but believed he'd be a great candidate for the Senate. At that time, Dan would owe Marco and his boss a lot of favors. Therefore, he would do whatever it took, very carefully, to ensure nothing would taint Dan's image.

Marco awoke at eight expecting basic information on a guy or two Ella had randomly picked up so he could pay them off or find a way to scare them from ever getting near her again. He did not expect to hear what players both of these men turned out to be. He was impressed by Ella's skills. After reading the file, it looked like she was definitely connected intimately to one, Chase O'Leary. The other, Clay Dixon, must have been his friend. Marco had great Vegas connections and knew he would have to work some magic here. He also needed to be careful that Chase did not associate with Marco's own contacts because of his role within the casinos. He called Dan at nine o'clock.

"What the hell is she doing with a casino consultant? I saw the fucking pictures, Marco. I've never known her to gamble in her life. She looks hot, fun, happy, and drunk! Damn, if she'd done that when we were married, maybe I would have had only half the women!"

"Dan, what do you want me to do? It's pretty touchy because of both these men's positions, not to mention their likeability and respect factors out here."

"Pretty sure you know what needs to happen. I want Ella left undamaged if possible. I'd like to make sure she's not some sort of lost twin first. What name did you hear she was going by these days? Janie?"

With a sigh, Marco said he'd talk to a few people and make sure there were not any leaks. These were the extreme sticky situations Marco hated. He was only glad that Dan seemed interested in keeping Ella away from harm. He genuinely liked her as a person and thought her the best front for Dan. She would help provide his ticket into the big league of politics if there was a remote chance of this going smoothly.

Just as he was sitting in the lobby chair reading the paper, he saw Ella come out of the elevator in jogging shoes, pants, and a blue Du Monde tank top. Marco thought she had a sexy, petite figure and couldn't help noticing her long legs, firm breasts, and nice ass. With her hair up in a ponytail and a faint smile on her face, she did not look like a depressed or angry woman who had just lost her mother or found her husband in bed with someone else. He kept his face behind the paper and admired her as she walked out the door. Dan was an idiot, but Marco would enjoy keeping an eye on her for him.

Chapter 23

CONNECTED DOTS

E mbarrassment and guilt overcame Janie. She could not stop shaking on the elevator ride down from the penthouse. Of course, she had been scared as hell. Clay Dixon pulled a Jekyll-Hyde move on her. His switch from a carefree, fun guy looking to impress her turned very sinister and controlling in a matter of seconds. She'd never experienced anyone like that before and certainly not so close to his room. She had way too many drinks earlier and was in no condition to fight back with any conviction. To top it off, Chase came to her rescue just in time, even though she was sure he thought she was angry at him. In the end, she did not even have much information for him. She felt like an absolute idiot.

Chase was at a loss for words. He put her in such a horrible situation and knew she must have felt she owed it to him to gather information. He had no idea what an asshole this guy was with women, and he was sure Dixon had found a good reason to lure her up to his room. There was no doubt in his mind that had he not come at that precise moment, Dixon would have raped her within minutes. He was speechless but held her close to him in the elevator. He led her to another elevator toward his suite. As they approached it, Chase opened the door. Once they were inside, he faced Janie and took both her hands in his. She looked up at him with tears filling her blue eyes, making them look like bright turquoise gems in a pool of water.

"Janie, I am so sorry for all of this. I can get another room and sleep somewhere else tonight to give you . . ."

Without letting him finish his sentence, she put her arms around his neck and pulled his face to hers, saying nothing and kissing him hard on the lips. Chase could taste the salt from her tears and kissed her back fervently. Without interrupting their intense kiss, he picked her up and laid her down on the bed. He was sure she had no worries about him being like Dixon, therefore he opted not to treat her like a porcelain doll that might break. It had been three days of serious foreplay in which their attraction for each other had intensified to the point at which a balloon blows up and up and up and may pop at any moment. Within seconds, her dress was off, beads and sequins flying across the room. Janie's heart was racing as if she'd had a huge shot of adrenaline. She could hardly breathe, but there wasn't anything unpleasant about the situation. She smiled at Chase as he tried to compose himself slightly and take a tiny bit more time with the lacy bra. He cupped a firm, round breast and kissed her while pulling off the delicate thong as she gracefully bent her long, limber legs through, maximizing her vulnerability.

She looked up at Chase, who was still fully dressed in his bow tie, tuxedo shirt, and pants. At that moment, she did not care about anything but getting his pants off. Janie reached for the button and undid the zipper. Chase quickly tore off his pants and ripped off his shirt and bow tie, managing not to choke himself. With one more deep kiss, he had no doubt Janie was ready for him. There wasn't any more foreplay this time as he entered her. She gasped in pleasure and looped her arms under his to feel his warm body against her as they moved together in unison. He waited as long as he could before coming and was sure it was mutual.

Janie finally breathed out a few times. She was certain this was the most exciting sex she'd ever had—and with such unbelievable chemistry.

She shuddered in pleasure and was soon ready for more. Chase did not disappoint her. By the end of the night and into the morning, they had tried multiple positions and tasted just about every inch of each other. At 4 a.m., they finally broke the spell of silence. They both felt like they'd been talking, just in another language.

"I don't know anything about you, yet you are the most amazing woman I have ever met, Janie Blue. With that, I am giving you a good-night kiss, as I have an early morning meeting at which I will be extremely tired." He laughed. "But I *will* still have a smile on my face thinking of you." He lightly kissed the hollow area of her neck just between her clavicles and traced his finger downward.

With a mischievous smile on her face, Janie whispered smugly, "After that, I may actually have to call you Ace."

They both passed out exhausted.

Seven came way too early. The hotel phone rang loudly and Chase grabbed it as quickly as possible so as not to wake Janie. His efforts had worked as he looked over and saw her long, black hair, perfectly messed up, covering her face and one breast as she slept peacefully. This woman did not have a bad moment, he thought. She looked like someone out of a French painting from long ago. He hated to leave her but wrote a note and called to make sure breakfast, flowers, and coffee would be delivered at ten. He left the note on the pillow next to her, saying:

Good AM, Sleeping Beauty—

There is a massage with your name on it at the spa. They are expecting you. They also have comfortable clothes to choose from if you'd like to take a walk and explore while I'm in this meeting. I should be out around two. I have another quick meeting later and I'd like you to come with me.

Afterward, will you join me for dinner and a show?

—Chase

Chapter 24

A MOMENT OF BLISS

Janie woke up just as there was a soft knock at the door. Feeling disheveled, she threw on a robe, paying little attention to the state of the room, and went to the door.

It was the same young guy from yesterday, politely trying not to smile and saying, "Good morning, miss. I hope I didn't wake you."

"Of course not, I was just getting up. What do you have there . . . um . . . Jake?" as she squinted tiredly with a playful grin at his silver name tag.

He rolled in the table with fresh lilacs and said, "Breakfast, mademoiselle. Croissants, French press coffee, and a succulent bowl of fresh raspberries. Sent by Mr. O'Leary, of course."

"It looks wonderful, Jake. Thank you." With that, she ran over to the corner of the room where her purse fell last night. She shook his hand and tipped him with a poker chip. "Afraid that's all I have. Sorry it's not cash."

Jake was used to being tipped with chips and not cash and knew all about the dollar amounts of every color. She tipped him a $100 chip. "Miss, that is way too much. Do you know the value?"

"Jake, my name is Janie, and you deserve it for seeing this mess and me so early in this state. Thanks again. Now have a great day!"

Jake thanked her and left knowing that he could put it toward the car he needed to fix. Today, he loved his job and thought Chase was a very lucky guy.

The mixture of lilacs and French press coffee smelled fantastic. Janie poured the coffee into the large white mug and added a touch of cream and the cinnamon provided. This was exactly what she needed. She felt genuinely relaxed and happy. Knowing Chase had a meeting this morning, she wondered if he left her a note. Comfortably predictable, he had left it on the pillow. She liked what he said and thought a massage and walk sounded wonderful. She didn't want to think any more ahead or read more into it, as Janie thought she would savor what she had at this moment and enjoy herself. Being pampered was a wonderful thing for any girl, she thought.

Janie called down to the spa. They informed her to come down and encouraged her to wear the robe. The elevator from her suite would take her directly to the spa floor. After drinking her coffee, taking a few bites of a croissant and the delicious berries, Janie jumped in the hot shower to rinse off for her massage. She cut it short, thinking how she almost fell apart the last time she took a shower here. Throwing on the robe, she quickly looked both ways out the suite door and bolted for the elevator. The doors opened directly to a serene spa set in tones of light blue, sea green, and pale gray with heated limestone floors. It was both modern and timeless.

Almost immediately, a young woman in a white T-shirt with light-blue letters depicting "Spa Du Monde" greeted her. She led her to a massage room. Janie lay down on the heated massage table and had drifted off to sleep by the time the therapist put the hot towels on her back. She gave Janie an extra half-hour massage to let her sleep. Chase was a great client and a heavy tipper, so she wanted to do everything possible to make sure Miss Blue had a relaxing experience. She gently woke her up.

"Miss Blue, I hope you feel nice and relaxed. Please take as much time as you'd like. Mr. O'Leary said you may be going for a walk, so I took the liberty of leaving a few of our yoga pants and one pair of stretch pants as well as a choice of T-shirts, socks, and tennis shoes. I hope they are to your liking."

"They all look perfect. I'll just try them on, Marina, and see which fits. Is there a size 8 shoe in there somewhere?"

"Yes. As your massage therapist, I got a pretty good look at your feet and guessed correctly."

"Thank you. I'll be out in a jiffy."

Janie immediately picked the black, flared yoga pants, a light aqua, loose-fitting racer-back tank, and a Lululemon white jog bra. The Adidas shoes were almost blindingly white, but they fit her narrow feet and felt comfortable. That was that. Janie was off to explore the city and couldn't keep her thoughts off of Chase. As an added bonus, she found ten poker chips totaling a thousand dollars in her purse. Her first thought was that the sick bastard Dixon had given her the first $100 to bet at blackjack, but then quickly recounted his actions later that evening and thought she would spend the money without guilt on a small shopping spree.

Sunlight poured in as the elevator opened to the lobby. She made a mental note to buy new sunglasses. Janie was ready to take a walk toward the Bellagio and shop a little along the way. She needed a few necessities and something cute for this evening. In her daydreamy state, Janie walked right by Marco, her husband's right-hand man, without so much as a glance.

Chapter 25

LET'S MAKE A DEAL

As Chase walked into the meeting, O'Shea, Jax, and Clay Dixon were waiting for him. Chase knew he was a few minutes late, but he had needed the extra sleep. He focused on fully comprehending the complexity and nuances of this meeting in order to make any important decisions. He knew they would want answers on the spot and he must be prepared to give them.

Upon his entrance, Dixon walked up first to shake his hand. Under his breath, he muttered, "Looks like your talk went well last night, Chase. I had a great night, thanks to you, but I have to admit I was a bit envious. Hope we can start off fresh today."

Chase bit the inside of his cheek and nodded his head. He shook Clay's hand solidly and looked him squarely in the eyes with his Paul Newman squint. He said nothing directly in return, instead focusing on the others.

"Jax, O'Shea, Dixon, sorry I am a bit late. There was a little line at the café this morning, and it was a long night last night. You make it very difficult to go to bed early here with my favorite pastime."

They all laughed. Jax and O'Shea both knew of his love of poker, and Dixon knew exactly what he was talking about. O'Shea started in by discussing his long alliances with all of them and his complete trust in their areas of expertise as well as their knowledge of this casino.

He leaned forward as they sat at a small, round mahogany table in his private office and sighed, saying, "I also know from experience and years of watching all of you closely that none of you would betray me in any way, even if you choose not to participate in my very intriguing and lucrative proposal."

In describing the intricacies of the hotel and the numbers of visitors versus its expenses in today's economy, especially with the ominous threat of Y2K on the horizon, Chase knew which direction this discussion was taking. He was originally hired by Global Insurance to assess the risk and viability of Du Monde. If he thought the risk too great through a high degree of proof, he would be awarded a percentage of the potential loss of the claim. However, he had no faith in the insurance company and thought them to be stiff asshole wannabes. Their good old boys' network was just that. They were a bunch of boys sitting around not willing to do the work themselves. He took this job as a safety net to identify a niche for himself, knowing all the while where his allegiances lay. Chase grew up in the South Side of Chicago and knew the value of a dollar and the connections from which the money came.

He needed to make this work and explain his undercover job to O'Shea when they took a break. O'Shea knew Mac from Chase's past. Chase met O'Shea when he was a kid and O'Shea ran a much smaller casino. Both had been successful and done favors for each other for a long time. He knew Tom O'Shea and thoroughly trusted him or he wouldn't be sitting across the table from him now. He was also pretty sure he was going to ask all of them to heist his casino or partially destroy it, leading, of course, to insurance fraud. Either way, he needed to stay as far away from the event as possible and find a way to explain this without losing his credibility.

Chapter 26

A MATTER OF TRUST

O' Shea went on to address his "gang": "Jax, you know the employees, the clients, the who's who, and the ins and outs of this place better than anyone. You've seen every plan of this hotel and then some before it was built. Clay, your expertise lies in codes and numbers. Chase, your security knowledge is better than anyone's in the business, which is why I haven't hired you for this hotel. By now, you are all getting an idea of what I'm saying. Let's take a break for coffee. I will discuss what I want from each of you one time only. If you should say yes, I'll be ecstatic. If it's a no, we have all known each other a long time. There are bonds and trust on the line. But I am sure none of them will be crossed. Let's meet back here in ten minutes. Coffee is in the conference room."

Dixon and Jax nodded and walked to the conference room. Chase took this opportunity to talk with O'Shea privately. He didn't have long and needed to sound sure of his words and thoughts. Before speaking, Chase took a moment.

"Something on your mind, Ace? You know you can speak freely

with me or you wouldn't be here. Of any of these guys, I know exactly where you came from and how much you can be trusted."

"Tommy, I'm not going to beat around the bush on this one. I've known you a long time and my ties to you, Billy, and Mac are not to be reckoned with. I was approached a year ago by Global Insurance. In your recent dealings, of course, you know them well. You should be bound in two days' time by them if given my approval on your risk factor. I have wanted to get in with them for many reasons. They are the main insurance company to bind luxury hotels and casinos around the world. They have very little knowledge of my past associations or tight personal connections in Chicago or here in Vegas. They think I am a successful security specialist trying to make as much money as possible with the best-paying casinos in Las Vegas or anywhere, for that matter. Since I came here, I've been trying to figure out a way to legally help my colleagues without any real strings. My financial security has always been taken care of generously, so of that I am not so concerned. This is it, Tommy. I am sure we have an understanding. In two days, upon my go-ahead, your casino will have a significant policy with a highly respected company, Global Insurance. However, I will need to steer clear of your casino to whatever capacity you plan on any activities arising in a future claim. Down the road, I would be thrilled to work with you on your newly updated security measures as your number one security specialist. Are we clear on this?"

Tom O'Shea had a great poker face when he wanted. Chase knew it all too well but waited until he broke into a grin.

With a low, husky laugh, he slowly shook his head from side to side saying, "Ace, you are my hundred-million-dollar man. When I get the policy signed off, there will be a nice sum in your special offshore account. Global deserves this with how they mishandled Mac's fire at the pool hall twenty years ago, right? They've become the best, but I'll feel no guilt because of their typical back-stabbing insurance-company behavior. When you see Billy later, let him know whether all went as planned. He'll get the message to me, and you and your gal will have a very nice bottle of champagne to celebrate. We'll catch up later. Check your other account in three days. Why don't you do what you need to do now, and I'll let these guys know a different plan is in place. What else can I say, Ace?"

"Got it, Tommy. I'd better move on this. You need to do what is best for Du Monde. It's a great place, and I'd like to help you with it in the future. I'll be out of here tomorrow and in touch only through Billy after that." He shook Tom O'Shea's hand, and they gave each other a quick, hearty hug.

They trusted and respected each other, knowing that each had the capacity to do his job. Chase gave a nod and was gone. Now, he needed to give a convincing report to his liaison at Global Insurance. The guy was actually an insider wannabe twit who tried to imitate the undercover guys from various television shows he had seen. Chase was certain that *CSI* was where this guy had acquired any of his knowledge or lingo. He was a piece of work. It would actually please Chase to play with him like he was a mouse: offer him his favorite cheese and walk him straight into a trap. He knew exactly what to say and the deal would be done.

After satisfying his pushover insurance contact and certain they would bind Du Monde, Chase wondered how Janie was faring. He had to keep her from his mind so he could stay focused, but now she was all he could think of. As he entered the casino, he called up to the room. No answer. Most people went for a walk in Vegas thinking everything looked to be about a block away, not realizing the scale of these hotels and the length of time it would take to get there. She was pretty energetic. She probably thought she could get through them all in two or three hours. It was three. He knew he said two on the note, so he thought he'd check with the desk and see if anyone had seen her lately. Just then, he bumped into Jake, his favorite go-to guy for room service.

"Hey there, Jake, was she up when you delivered?"

"Sure was, Mr. O'Leary. She seemed happy to get the flowers

and very happy for the coffee."

"Any sign of Miss Blue?"

As nonchalantly as possible, he replied, "Uh . . . well . . . I think I just saw her at the blackjack table."

"Which one?"

"One hundred."

Chase tried not to laugh, but thanked Jake with a twenty spot and headed for the tables. As he walked into the casino area, the air grew colder as the air conditioner was on high while the oxygen pumped through the vents, keeping everyone awake to play. There were no windows as usual so as to block out time, and the *ching-ching-ching* of the slots made you feel alive. It was every novice gambler's dream to close their eyes, pull that handle down hard, and beat the odds to hear the bells go off for the big million-dollar win. Most would be happy with a hundred dollars. It was the thrill of the game, really.

Well, there she was. With a pile of chips and a smile on her face, flirting with the dealer. In yoga pants, tank top, and a ponytail no less. Still, she looked stunning. He snuck up on her as she waved her hand over the cards to stay.

He whispered in her ear, "I would have chanced it and taken the next card, miss."

She turned around, forgetting about her hand and the table as she planted a kiss on his lips. "I'm so sorry, Chase, what time is it? I've been having so much fun, I completely forgot about the time."

The dealer knew Chase but tried to act professionally. "Miss, house wins. Sorry."

"Looks like you won a lot more than you lost. Time to cash in? This is precisely how people become addicted gamblers, Janie. I'll have to keep an eye on you. Why don't you cash in and I'll meet you in the room. I have one quick errand to run and will be up in thirty minutes."

"I'll see you then. I missed you this morning but enjoyed the special treatment. The spa is amazing here."

He playfully smacked her tight butt as she turned to go and she acted in fun as though it didn't happen. Chase knew exactly where to go. He walked quickly to the eclectic jewelry store within the hotel. The manager came right over, ready to show him something beautiful and expensive. It wasn't that he wouldn't, but he was looking for something else that was fun and had meaning. And . . . there it was in the case of sterling silver charms. Chase found a silver ace card and a tiny slot machine. He thought Janie would get a kick out of this. He would start her a charm bracelet to remind her of her soul searching, if that's what it was, in Vegas. It would also remind her of him and her newly acquired gambling skills. He asked the obliging manager to wrap it up in a turquoise-blue velvet pouch with a pull string.

As Chase sauntered to the lobby, he noticed that the same guy was sitting in the same chair reading the *USA Today* that he had been reading earlier. He quickly glanced his way to get a good look at his face. He was on edge after his meetings earlier even though he felt both went off without a hitch and he was in the clear. It reminded him of his earlier days in Chicago, looking over his shoulder constantly. Deciding to blow it off, Chase pondered about seeing Janie. He opened the hotel room door and heard the shower running. Perfect timing, he thought, and went into the bathroom, hoping to join her.

Upon entering the steam-filled bathroom, he immediately got undressed. He did not care about being presumptuous. He was pretty sure the feeling would be mutual.

He saw her petite silhouette in the shower and could no longer resist. Opening the door, he noticed she momentarily flinched and then smiled at him seductively.

"Nice timing. I was hoping you'd join me if you made it back."

"Wouldn't have missed this for any meeting. You may be the only woman who could look even better with a wet head and no makeup at all. You are truly stunning, Janie. I'm a lucky guy."

"So I've heard, Ace." She said sarcastically. "Now come over here and feel how smooth my skin is from that spa treatment. She grabbed his hands and pulled him closer to her.

After their shower, both emerged refreshed and relaxed.

"I hope you don't mind visiting a friend with me before our night out," Chase said. "I'll make it quick. He's got some information. We'll be meeting up with Billy, Blake's boss from the Pioneer Bar. Apparently, he had such great things to say about you that Billy put you on his 'must meet' list."

"I would love to accompany you to all of the above," she said with a lot more confidence than she felt inside. When he mentioned Billy, something made Janie consciously uncomfortable.

Chapter 27

WHY BILLY?

Unsure as to why she had a knot in her stomach at the thought of meeting Billy Martinelli, Janie tried to shrug off her worries and focus on her date. She began telling Chase about the money she won and her trivial shopping adventure. She slipped on a casual off-the-shoulder, navy-blue Susana Monaco jersey dress. It fell way above the knee, showing off her great legs. She had bought some bronzing foam earlier to even out her tan and picked up a pair of strappy leather heels and small, gold hoop earrings. Her makeup was minimal and fresh, and she let her hair go natural and wavy. It suited her perfectly.

In his khakis and soft white button-down, Chase looked good enough to take back to the shower and start over. He could not get enough of her either and decided to hand her his little token.

"Oh, I picked this up earlier. I wanted to remind you of me," he said very seriously.

"Oh no . . . now, I am feeling really guilty. I went on a shopping spree and didn't buy you anything."

"Believe me when I say you are the best gift any man could receive."

She pulled on the bag's strings and took out the delicate charms. As she saw what they were, she let out a relieved, happy laugh and told him she would absolutely cherish them.

"These are the two best charms I have ever received. It will always keep you around my wrist, Ace, and remind me not to get into too much trouble with my new gambling habit!"

"I'll have the bracelet tomorrow. I wanted you to go in and have them size it and pick your style."

She held the charms in both hands, bringing her clasped hands to her lips and quickly kissed them. She placed the delicate slot machine and ace into the small pocket in her dress and promised not to lose them. Next, she brushed his lips with a kiss as she could tell they'd never get out of the room to his meeting if she went any further.

Chase's phone vibrated and he said, "I think that's our car waiting downstairs."

He had decided to borrow one of the casino's BMWs so they could ride comfortably on this hot, windy evening. Summers in Vegas usually meant a hundred-plus degrees and often very dusty windstorms. Janie was impressed, joking that he looked too serious in this car. All the while she was thrilled to have a top on and air conditioning in this heat wave.

They talked easily on the drive over to Billy's. It was forty-five minutes away, as there was quite a bit of traffic at this hour. He finally had to ask her a couple of questions because he truly wanted to know more about her. He had never felt this way or had this much chemistry with any woman, yet he knew nothing about her past. He knew he needed to give her space, but craved more. He did not want to go around her to find out.

"So, Janie Blue, you really have kept a low profile, you know. I have a couple of simple questions for you: Where are you from, and who are you looking for or hiding from here in Vegas?" He said this with a serious tone, and the car was silent.

Janie sucked in her breath, lost her smile, and quietly told him,

"I don't know the answer to those questions today. I am learning a lot about myself right now—can you accept this for the moment? Besides, I haven't asked anything of you, not even where we are going or why. I mean, how did you get into this casino world in the first place?"

"For now, I will go with the line that you are 'finding yourself' and will tell you my life in a nutshell. I grew up in Chicago and was raised by a very Catholic mother and a tough, alcoholic police officer for a father. Most of my teen years were spent around a pool hall. I did a short stint in jail at eighteen and don't want that life back. However, I have strong connections to very connected people who need information. I am happy to provide that information 'legally,' for a price. My loyalty does not waiver, and I was definitely raised with Catholic guilt and ties that bind for life. The rest you see is who I am, Janie."

Janie listened as if receiving a special gift. She was sure he did not talk about his past to many and felt very guilty and embarrassed that she could not talk about her past or her reason for the lack of discussion. She really did not know the answers, but had no intention of letting him in on her confusion.

"Thank you, Chase, for being so open with me. You are very special and . . ." Janie drifted as she looked out the window as if she recognized this street. Her mouth opened slightly while she stared at the odd familiarity surrounding this place. Her head began to spin and her fingers felt tingly as her breathing became shallow.

Chase saw Billy's car over by the small house. This neighborhood was a great place for young couples and starter homes back in the day, about twenty or twenty-five years ago. Slowly, it changed. Now it was not a place you'd want to raise kids or even be in after dark. He couldn't figure out why Billy wanted to meet here except that it was definitely out of the way. The cops didn't even like frequenting it as much as they should.

"Well, here we are. Why don't you wait in here for a minute. I need to have a word with Billy alone. Afterward, I will introduce you."

He couldn't figure out her reserved behavior as they neared the house but thought maybe it was fear she had as this place was pretty rough and kind of scary to someone who didn't grow up around here. How wrong he was in his thoughts, but he quickly assured her he'd be right back and just over by the black car ahead.

Chase went to shake Billy's hand and realized Billy was not even looking at him but over Chase's left shoulder instead. After Chase left the car, Janie walked slowly and dreamily toward the house as if mesmerized. She knew this home from her dreams, and now it was real. Down to the white turned posts and three steps leading to the small porch. Now the paint was peeling and cracking and the house looked abandoned and neglected. She felt faint and took hold of the stair railing as flashes flooded her mind. She saw the mother in her dreams, a small child, a birthday cake with candles, a white puppy barking one minute then bloody and dead another. The last flashes brought her to her knees. They were of her mother, Eliza Jane, lying on the floor and a man whose face was deeply cut in the form of the letter Y. Janie was shaking uncontrollably.

Chapter 28

REWIND

Billy saw her walking over to the house. It had been her home a long time ago. She was the spitting image of his lost love, Lizzie, with longer hair. As Chase walked up, Billy heard nothing of what he was saying.

Billy whispered hoarsely, "Chase, how did you come to meet Janie?"

"Why are you so interested in her, Billy? What is going on here?"

"Stay here for a minute, Chase. I need a minute with her."

Chase did not like the look in his eye nor his interest in Janie. He turned to look over his shoulder and saw her in front of the house supporting her weight by leaning on an old, dilapidated post. He moved to run over to her, and Billy stopped him.

"I mean it, Chase, let me handle this. Just give me a minute alone with her. Trust me."

In saying this, Billy walked quickly over to Janie and watched her fall to her knees.

He got down on his knees and lifted her chin. "It's really you, Janie, isn't it? You look so much like your mother. Do you remember me?

Will you listen to me, please? I don't want to make you forgive me, just understand that your mother was the love of my life. I was an addict and crazy with paranoid delusions. I . . ."

Janie looked at his still scarred cheek and with all the strength she could muster, she smacked his face with the heel of her hand.

Through clenched teeth, she said shakily, "You are the man from my nightmares, and now I know I wasn't crazy. You killed my mother and changed my life forever. Rot in hell!" She got off her knees and ran as fast as she could away from the house.

Chase ran over right away and grabbed Billy. He knew she wouldn't get too far, and he needed to find out what the hell had just happened.

"Billy, what in the hell is going on here? How do you know Janie, and what did you say to her?"

Billy felt sick as his feelings of remorse came flooding back. With tears in his eyes, he said, "Go after her. This is a shitty neighborhood, Chase. Her mother was Lizzie."

Chase was stunned and let him go. He had no idea how this had gotten so twisted. Did she know this all along, or was this a very strange coincidence? He ran in the direction she had gone but could no longer see her. It was starting to get dark. He knew she could not have run very far. As he looked around, he realized he was behind a shop of some sort. He saw a concrete stairwell leading down to a basement. Looking below, he recognized Janie, but she was sitting on the cold, dirty concrete floor at the bottom of the stairs with her arms around her knees and her head down, sobbing. He rushed down the stairs, taking them two at a time to get to her as fast as he could.

He put his arms around her, but she did not respond. He raised his voice to get her to snap out of it: "Janie! You okay? What just happened with Billy? Talk to me, dammit!"

In a state of emotional meltdown, Janie very much knew what was happening at the moment. She just needed to process the information. What she didn't need was this man she was falling for involved in her recurring nightmares. At the same time, she wanted some information about him. Did he knowingly arrange this meeting with that murderer? Did he care about her, or was she just some pawn in a game? She would not look up at Chase. Within minutes, Billy came rushing to the stairs.

He yelled to Chase, "Get up here! We have a serious situation and I need you up here right now!"

Chase was torn between calming Janie and punching Billy in the face. However, the urgency in his voice was not to be taken lightly. Billy was one cool, collected guy who had been around and was highly respected. He ran back up the stairs, keeping an eye on Janie the entire time.

"Chase, something is very wrong here. We have time to discuss this fucked-up emotional dilemma with Janie later. Right now, I just received an alarming call from one of my best informants. Word on the street is that someone placed a hit on you. I am trying to find out who as we speak. I don't believe it is O'Shea. He cannot praise you enough for helping him out with Global. Do you think the insurance company has gotten wind of this?"

He did not believe the insurance company could be involved, yet right now he could not be so sure of anything. The last twenty-four hours had not been anything he had expected.

"Jesus, Billy. I can tell you think this information comes from a good source, but I have no idea what to think. I will get her out of here. Have someone you trust meet me with my Jeep out past Summerlin behind the theater building that's for lease. I know where to go. I'll use my secondary phone number, okay? As soon as you find out who is behind this, let me know."

"Chase, we will find this guy. Just get her somewhere safe. She and her mother were the closest thing I ever had to a family. I want to talk to her again."

Getting Janie out of there was easier said than done. She was a furious mess. He had no idea how strong she was until he tried to pick her up and carry her to the car unwillingly. All the while she hit, kicked, and yelled.

"You bastard, Chase! Now does your 'boss' want me dead too? I refuse to go with you! Leave me the hell alone!"

He hated doing it, but for her own safety and his ability to drive safely in a likely car chase with hit men, he knocked her out and loathed himself for it. If she awoke ready to jump or fight, it would take her some time to do so. There was really nothing else he could do; getting to safety was essential. She had been out of control with a crazed look on her face. When Billy saw him carrying her limp body, he ran over to Chase.

"I had to knock her out, Billy. She was going nuts. She'll be fine. I'll be in Summerlin in thirty minutes if I take the back roads. We'll work this out later, okay? Just so you know, I'm falling in love with this woman. I will not let anything happen to her, got it?"

Billy knew he had no right to worry or hope he could have any relationship with Janie, but he wanted to make sure she was safe and find out which corner of the world she came from. He had been searching for her since Child Services had taken her away. For some reason, he could not find out anything about her adoption. He thought maybe the FBI had put her in witness protection. Later, it seemed the system had simply lost her.

Now, he kept calling all of his resources. Someone had to know something out there. Who were these guys, and why Chase? His phone rang: a call from Blake. Blake always had information.

"Blake, what's going on?"

"Billy, no one's talkin'. Somewhere in the Du Monde, there was a USA Today found with two names on it: Chase and Janie. We are sure it was left by the guy sent to watch them. Do you think this could mean there is a hit on both of them? And, why?"

Billy was ready to dial Chase and warn him but didn't need to worry him more. He would also meet in Summerlin, a suburb of Vegas, himself to take Janie to safety and try to find out more. The unknowns here were huge. Who were these guys? And did they know the whereabouts of Janie and Chase at this moment?

Chapter 29

PREVAILING CHAOS

Finally, the call came. Dan, Ella's husband, could not go out to Las Vegas and confront the situation; he had to keep up appearances and escape any potential involvement. This whole thing was extremely touchy and could kill his career, if not land him in prison for life by association.

Marco, Dan's informant, spoke in a hushed voice as he told Dan the news. "We are having Ella, and this guy, Chase, followed and have a plan of action. It looks like Ella may be in the middle of a mess herself and not such an eager participant. The man she is with has some interesting friends of whom we need to steer clear, but they could also provide us with easy scapegoats if we choose to take care of this problem the way you were thinking."

"What do you mean Ella is in trouble? I thought she looked like she was having a good time out there, last we talked."

"I was mistaken. One of my guys just saw her in a very seedy part of town. They saw her running from two men, punched in the face, and thrown into a car. Maybe we should listen to her story before deciding to give her the same fate as Chase. I have a plan that may work to keep her out of the way of police, the public, or hospitals. It may not go perfectly, so I cannot promise you anything, but I'll do my best, okay?"

Marco did not want Ella's blood on his hands—no way! He would basically act like it was Dan's own idea to spare her. If he didn't, then Marco would make Dan actually say it and not just imply what he wanted done. Dan would need to feel the guilt and shame of that move on his own. In other words, Dan would have to kill her himself.

"It had better be a good plan, Marco. I'll stand by. Call me as soon as you have anything. I am going to make sure I am seen now at a meeting in Seattle to discuss running for Senate."

Marco thought his plan was working beautifully. Billy Martinelli, the casino insider, seemed to be heading in the same direction as Chase. After a while, Marco was informed that they were slowing down in a fairly deserted area behind an old theater. They could send these guys in and make it look like a mafia- or gang-related disagreement. Everyone knew Billy and, from what he was hearing, they also knew Chase.

As Chase showed up, he saw his Jeep with the keys inside and no one else around. Within seconds, Billy showed up.

"Chase, you get the hell out of here, now! I'll take Janie to a safe house in Mount Charleston until I can get more information. I think she may be in trouble by association with you. We saw her name on what we think was a hit list."

He was about to object to Billy when a shot was fired at the BMW where Janie lay passed out. Billy and Chase were running to Janie when bullets started flying from all directions. They could not get to her and had to get the attention away from the car. Billy was hit but managed to get in his car, and Chase fled the area in his Jeep with a pop to the left shoulder. They had to lead these guys away from Janie. Chase shifted into high gear and made it to Red Rock as a car followed him. He wasn't far ahead of these guys, but far enough to think of the next move. Chase headed for a drop-off he knew well. He saw them behind and knew only one way to truly get them off his back. He just hoped his plan worked.

Billy had others following him yet managed to lose them by going into his friend's warehouse where he kept many "unregistered" cars. In thirty seconds, he emerged with a different car and went straight back to the scene to see what was happening from afar. He was not close enough to see if Janie was okay. An ambulance and a police car had arrived at the scene already. Within a minute, he saw the EMT shaking his head as he put a sheet over her head and lifted her body into the ambulance. Billy was heartbroken. He could not contain his gut-felt yell that was so loud he was surprised the men below did not hear him. Now, he had to find out if Chase was okay and break the devastating news to him. As the ambulance drove off without sirens, so did Billy. He frantically called a few of his associates, seeing if anyone had made it over toward Red Rock in the direction Chase was heading. He had faith in Chase's abilities and quick reactions, but these assholes were right on his tail. In all of the commotion, Billy had almost forgotten he'd been hit, skimmed really. But now it was beginning to hurt like hell.

Knowing that the car was far enough away but close enough to see him go over the cliff, Chase thought quickly. He grabbed the heavily loaded backpack and put it on the gas pedal as soon as he started going over the first embankment. He jumped out when he knew they could not see him. As he rolled, he looked to see the taillights of his Jeep go over the cliff. In his adrenaline-rushed state, he stealthily moved behind huge rocks. He knew this canyon well and would easily find his way out without them finding any trace of him.

Besides, Chase had no doubt that after hearing the explosion of his car and the depth to which it fell, they would write him off for good.

Chapter 30

A PLAN

A lthough it was just a sedative they gave her to knock her out, the doctor was concerned about his lovely patient's outcome. Her breathing was not normal, her blood pressure too low, and she seemed to be having some sort of seizure. He never liked getting a call from Marco Diego. He owed him a favor this time and promised absolute secrecy. In a normal situation, this patient would be in a topnotch hospital having the irregular heart rhythms and gun-shot wound checked out. Everything was done accordingly, yet she was not responding the way he had hoped. He had fully expected her to be awake by now. He decided to grab a cup of coffee and prayed she would wake up soon so he could check her speech and vitals. As he left, a tall, dark-haired man passed him whom he vaguely recognized. They were in his clinic, which was closed for the evening, yet he had not seen him earlier. Marco Diego appeared just as Dr. Colter was about to stop Dan from entering his patient's room.

"Doc, he's cleared. How is she? Awake yet?"

"No response so far, Marco. It could be the trauma from the

'accident,' a result from the blow to her head, shock from her gunshot wound, or possibly the mix of harsh sedatives she was given," he added sarcastically.

Dan sat next to Ella, thinking that his wife was an extremely beautiful woman and wondered why he'd never seen her in that dress before.

"Ella, it's me, Dan. You okay, honey?" he whispered "sweetly" just in case she was awake. If she lived, he'd need to play the part of loving and caring husband. Thankfully, just then, the doctor entered and explained to Dan that his wife was out cold.

As he looked at her, he selfishly wanted her dead. His ego was so bruised by the fact that she was seen enjoying herself and having fun with another man that he could hardly stand it. He really didn't understand why Marco objected to killing her along with that idiot she was hanging out with. He understood that by his side, she would help his potential for getting elected, but he was also a narcissistic fool. In his mind, he felt his charisma and good looks qualified him to help run the country. For a brief moment, he looked around to see if anyone was watching. Part of him actually thought of pushing her dress up and showing her just who she could have fun with, while the other half of him wanted to do her in for good. He clenched his fist and just then, Marco walked in.

"He's out of the picture, Dan. Let's take a walk and talk as I'm not sure what kind of subconscious stuff goes on when people are out of it on sedatives."

Dan laughed and said, "You idiot, look at her. She's probably in a fucking coma. Quit acting like a superstitious child. Give me the details."

Marco explained to Dan that Chase was spotted in his Jeep driving over the cliff in Red Rock to his death. His guys had witnessed the whole thing. They were so close behind that their car almost went over while following him into the darkness.

"There was no way he could have lived from the height the car fell. They saw it crash to the bottom of a canyon and explode."

Under his breath, but in a rage, Dan said, "And just what the hell do you think she'll say when she wakes up, Marco? 'Dan, I've missed you so much. Now that I've had my fun, I'll be your perfect wife again.' Seriously, she should've been in the car with him, but then you think my numbers would go way down, right?"

"Pipe down, Dan. Let's just see what happens when she wakes up. There is always a plan B. Let's grab a drink." They walked down the dimly lit hallway.

About fifteen minutes later, Dr. Colter thought he heard some beeping from one of the monitors, so he went to check on his patient. She seemed to be coming to slowly. Her eyelids fluttered as she squinted from the light he had shone on her.

"You've had quite an accident, young lady. How do you feel?"

Chapter 31

THE MEMORY GAME

She sat up slowly and reached for the bowl next to her and vomited. She had no desire to speak and felt herself dying inside. Janie knew what she needed to do. For the last twenty-four hours, the reality of her transformation into Janie Blue had mixed with her past as Ella Ross and merged like a dream, drifting through her semi-conscious state. Hearing her pathetic excuse for a husband and Marco discuss what happened to Chase in such a cruel, unemotional way almost pushed her over the edge into hysterics. Luckily, the sedatives hadn't worn off just yet and she could hold back. Somehow, she would need to find the strength to wait and process his death when she was alone. Otherwise, Janie would not survive and never bring Dan to the justice he so deserved.

As her mind was churning and she stared blankly ahead, Janie heard the doctor's soft voice saying, "This is common from a concussion, Ella. You have a pretty nasty cut on your face and also a faint bruise on your forehead along with a gunshot wound on your leg. You've been out quite a while. You had us all a little worried."

He tentatively shined the light in her eyes and asked her a few questions to which she could not yet make herself respond. She knew what to do and would do her best to act the part of the victim.

Eventually, she managed to speak. "What happened to the car, doctor? I . . . I tried to avoid the deer on the way to my aunt's house and lost control. How did I get here? Is the car totaled? It was my mother's."

"Ella, do you know where you are? What city you are in?"

She put her hand to her head as if in pain and responded tentatively, "Well, I can't be far from my father's home as I drove only a couple hours before seeing the deer. I was stupid to take the country road instead of the main. Why do I feel like such a train wreck? My leg is throbbing like a huge chunk of glass is inside it. Did I go through the windshield?"

"Ella, you've been shot. Do you remember anything about Las Vegas?"

"What? My family has never taken me to Las Vegas. Why are you talking to me about Las Vegas? Where are Dan and my father? Have they been contacted? How was I shot? By a hunter after that deer I avoided?"

Dr. Colter thought better of saying anything more and did a few quick tests and moved the bed to a more upright position so he could examine his patient's motor functions better and assess her mental condition. He could tell from the answers to his questions that she remembered nothing of Las Vegas. He'd seen short-term memory loss like this before and long-term PTSD amnesia as well. He wanted her to have an MRI but also needed to talk with Marco to find out what really happened. The doctor owed him his life after serving in the Gulf War with him and would honor this favor of complete secrecy.

"Let me go and get your husband, okay? I'll be right back. Why don't you try to eat some of those ice chips."

Walking toward Marco and his friend, Dr. Colter felt like he needed to protect this woman. He wasn't sure what was going on here and needed to assess the situation carefully. He decided to make the diagnosis stronger than he actually felt.

"Listen, guys, she doesn't remember anything past having a car accident in Washington. She has no idea where she is at the moment. I think we need to take this slowly so as not to traumatize her with the details too quickly. However, in order to understand if I'm dealing with amnesia, I need to know more details of where she's been and what she has done. Also, more about her past medical and mental history. First, let's have you go see her, Dan. She was asking for you."

With that, Dan smiled slyly to Marco. At the same time, he was trying to think of what to say to her about the past week and what to eliminate.

Marco answered his unspoken questions by saying, "Dan, just play the role of the worried husband. Let her do the talking until we find out what we are dealing with. If it seems to be amnesia, you'll need to get Mike involved to get her childhood medical and mental history. I did a background check on her back before you married her and didn't see anything, but you might want to talk to him anyway."

Dan had never seen Ella look frightened and scared. She was not a very outgoing woman, but pleasant and reserved. Her lack of passion kept her very even-keeled and seemingly unbreakable. As he walked in, she bolted upright, which caused her a lot of pain. Dan instinctively ran over to her as if she were a wounded bird. He could see she'd been crying and wiped away her tears. He had seen her crying in private after her mother had died. When he approached her other times, she would simply wipe away her tears and talk of another subject. This was different. She was crying openly. What had started with a few tears opened the floodgates. He knew she needed him, and he felt like her hero. Dan put his arms around her and felt her passion. What he did not feel was her burning hatred for him.

"Ella, it's okay. What do you remember about the accident? You can talk to me. I'm here for you," he only half lied.

She was very convincing indeed. She knew her life depended on her actions and needed her head clear. Surely, she could mask her feelings by crying. In fact, the tears flowed so easily that she could not stop.

She gasped through her tears, "The deer . . . I swerved and must have hit it or a tree, but I just blacked out and felt nothing, nothing at all. Which hospital am I at? It's so quiet here. Has my dad been called? Dan, why was the doctor talking about Las Vegas and saying that I was shot? My head hurts so badly, I think I need to lie back down."

Dan helped her back down and gently brushed her long, wavy hair from her face. Something inside Dan wanted her more than ever at that moment. In her state, she needed him more than he needed her. Dan liked that feeling. Right now, he'd make the decision to tell Marco to give this a try and contact her father for more information. He kissed her forehead and said he'd get the doctor. His kiss felt like a sizzling brand to her skin. She hoped she would be able to keep this up long enough to gather enough information so he could rot in prison for the rest of his life.

Chapter 32

SAVED PAST

"**Y**ou're right, Doc. I've never seen her so upset or so confused. I'll call her father for more information, okay?"

Dan and Marco talked briefly. They decided it was best to let her father know that they found her hurt and in shock. They thought about saying it looked like she had been kidnapped and taken to Las Vegas, and it was a possible gang-related incident.

Just as Mike was walking back from outside, he heard his cell phone ring. He had left it on the island counter. Seeing Dan's number, he anxiously answered, "Dan, did you find her?" He prayed he would not hear the bad news he feared.

"She's with me, Mike. Hurt, but okay. I need you to . . ."

He interrupted, "Oh my God, where are you, Dan? I need to get there right now. Tell her I'm on my way."

"Hold on, Mike. This situation is very delicate in a number of ways. Ella has some sort of post-traumatic stress amnesia, the doctor says. He needs more information before we can move her. Also, we have to keep everything under control here. Let me give you some details and get you out here with a degree of secrecy. You can see Ella and meet with me and the doc first, okay?"

"The most important thing, Dan, is Ella's well-being. But, yes, I do not want an out-of-control media or anything getting misinterpreted here. Just tell me briefly what happened and answer a couple questions for me."

"It seems she was in an accident. At that point, someone kidnapped her for who knows what at the moment. She is physically fine except for a few cuts and bruises, but we are not sure why she cannot remember past the day she left for her aunt's house."

Mike thought for a long time. He'd never told anyone about just how Ella came to be their child, let alone the huge fact that she never remembered her life before them. For her sake, the dreaded day was here for him to discuss at length his weakness as a father.

Sadly, Mike recounted her childhood history to Dan, emphasizing that this amnesia had never recurred, but neither had her memories ever resurfaced from before the date they'd "adopted" her.

"Dan, I know this sounds crazy to you, but Kate and I were so desperate, and Ella's case was hopeless for the social worker at the time. They weren't sure how this child's mother was killed and wanted her to sort of disappear to a safe haven somewhere. All the stars seemed to align, and we gave her the best life we knew how to give a girl by surrounding her with everything a little girl could need." His voice was shaking over the phone.

Feeling like he had just won the jackpot in many ways, Dan listened carefully to what Ella's father had to say. This would explain her amnesia and possibly her reason for being in Las Vegas. Marco and Dan discussed the many possible reasons and went back and forth as to how much information to give the doctor.

Marco defensively told Dan, "I've known Jack Colter a long time and saved his life back in Iraq. He is as tight-lipped as anyone I know and very loyal. I think we need to tell him about her past so he can recommend some sort of treatment. We do not want her to remember her childhood past or this stint in Vegas. Let's see how that can happen, Dan. You need to trust me to do my job."

Dan agreed to discuss Ella with Dr. Colter, provided that they left out any hint of Ella's possibly being in Las Vegas of her own free will. They needed to stick strictly to the story of her potential abduction and involvement in this Vegas deal gone bad, just in case anything ever leaked out about her whereabouts. Also, they did not want to be seen as involved in a shoot-out near Summerlin. In actuality, it was their people shooting at Ella and her captors—or were they her friends? They'd definitely need to get to the bottom of that one. Dan would really like to believe that she had been held captive just like Marco had described.

Marco knew Dan needed to feel that Ella never had feelings for this guy, Chase, who went down in the accident. He, himself, did not know what really happened as he saw the pictures of her knocked out and carried over Chase's shoulder as he ran to the car. Maybe the jerk reeled her in with lies and was planning on killing her or was involved in a trafficking ring. For now, he would keep some of the images of Ella and Chase to himself and tell Dan he only saw her with him, but she did seem stressed. Maybe she was being blackmailed, he would say. For sure, he would leave out the day he saw her exiting the Hotel Du Monde unattended and looking happier and more carefree than he'd ever seen her before. As long as Dan's ego was stroked and he could keep his narcissistic urges under control, Marco believed Dan would be a successful politician and a strong ally. He had the charisma, brains, and good looks mixed with just the right amount of foolish desire that made him a perfect blackmail target for the future. He was a true actor and great orator whose confidence needed to be caressed to stay at high gear.

Several hours later, after a last-minute flight and a confusing drive to the clinic instead of a hospital like he would have expected, Mike stepped out of the car sent by Dan and walked quickly to the clinic door. He had called Dan about five minutes away as Dan had instructed so the doors would be open for him. As he entered the double doors, Dan greeted him and locked them behind as he escorted Mike to see his daughter. Walking through the dimly lit deserted hallway, Mike felt more like he were in a scene from a horror movie.

"I know you want to keep this quiet, Dan, but what the hell is going on here? Is Ella getting the treatment she needs? How did she get shot? Who is in charge?" He phrased these all with a threatening edge to his voice.

"You know that I'd have only the best people treating her, Mike. For God's sake, she's my wife!" He played the part of the offended and distressed husband well.

They both stared the other down for a moment until Mike's need to see his daughter overtook his suspicions concerning his ambitious son-in-law. He moved around Dan and asked while walking, "Which way to her room?"

"Mike, please wait until I have a minute to see her again and talk to her. I want to make sure she's prepared to see you. She's been pretty worked up. Just give me a few minutes."

Dan did not want to act suspicious but was a little worried what might be said. With a fair amount of certainty, he felt Ella would not remember Vegas at all. After his conversation with Dr. Colter, they decided to give her a pill that should more or less keep her past five days of trauma at bay. He wanted her to continue taking the pill, so they decided to tell Ella it was a different medication and label it accordingly so she would never become suspicious. This all made perfect sense—if everything went as planned. It was a strange case, but fortunately, our universe is constantly evolving and futures along with it. One change can wreak havoc or open one's eyes to the reality meant for them. So many theories have been written, and Ella was living proof chaos occurs. She had feigned sleep while Dr. Colter, Dan, and Marco met in the corner of her room, speaking quietly about the pills—but just loud enough for her to hear almost everything. All the while, she was creating an intelligent plan in her mind. Her first attempt at deceiving these men was to play the damsel in distress.

She knew that under no circumstances was she to discuss her understanding of the past five days if she wished to live. It seemed like a lifetime, but Ella needed to divert the pain she was feeling and mask it as something else. Of course, she was also upset about her mother Kate's sudden death. Her sadness was deepened with new memories of her biological mother Eliza Jane's tragic, brutal death. It seemed death followed her. She didn't want to believe Chase was gone, but she had to face the unbearable reality as she overheard everything Marco told Dan about the car exploding after a car chase. The sick reality of the lengths Dan would go to in the name of ambition and ego made her want to push him off into darkness. She thought some people should not have the privilege of living on this earth. His day would come. If she wasn't able to pull a trigger, then she'd make sure he suffered somehow.

Dan walked in to tell her that her father was worried sick about her and would be arriving soon. She simply cried, and even with the IV in her arm and tubes connecting her to machines, she buried her head in her arms so as not to look at him. Dan immediately caressed her hair in reaction to her emotional state.

"It'll be okay, Ella. The main thing is you are alive and fine with the exception of a few bumps and bruises. You were in an accident and robbed. We are going home and won't need to discuss this again if it bothers you, all right?"

"Dan, it's not me I am thinking about."

Chapter 33

A FINE LINE

At this Dan stiffened until he heard the rest of her sentence. "I am fine and can't seem to remember anything anyway. It's my mother. To me, I was just driving down to help with her memorial. I . . . I am just so sad about everything. I was never really able to understand her and had such a strained relationship with her. I will no longer be able to ask her why."

As Dan looked into her beautiful, sad eyes, he was sure he wanted her in his life. In fact, he liked this Ella a lot better than the perfect, slightly distant woman he knew before. Perhaps she would even be more appealing to the public. They always liked to see empathy, and that was something he had a hard time showing. According to Marco, he did not have a compassionate bone in his body.

Moments later, Mike walked in with a sad smile on his face and carefully hugged his sweet daughter. He was the polar opposite from her husband, she thought. How in the world did she end up with such a controlling jerk like Dan?

"Honey, I have been worried about you but should've known

better. You're a survivor and always have been. Sounds like you'll be out of here later today or tomorrow morning. We'll head home. How do you feel?" he asked carefully.

Although Ella wanted to cry, she needed to let him know she would be fine, especially since the love of his life had died only a week ago. She tried hard to give a little smile. "Dad, I just feel bad about the car—Mom's car, how is it? She would be so upset and is probably looking at us right now, saying, 'I told you not to let her drive my MG!'" Ella gave a weak laugh.

"That bumblebee is still a stinger, Ella. After a little work on the engine and repairs to a couple of dents, she'll be good as new. Besides, no one could have predicted a deer jumping in front of you. Do you remember anything, sweetie?" Like Dan, he really hoped she did not.

"Just seeing the deer and a bumpy ride through trees, then darkness," she said with as much sincerity as she could muster.

He hugged her again and said he'd let her rest and would figure out her discharge with Dan. Outside, he and Dan had discussed the idea of letting her know only about the accident and that she had been shot by a common thief who didn't want her walking anywhere and describing him to the local police until he was far away. They thought it better to pretend they were never in Las Vegas so as to avoid memories of her past here as a child. Mike was unsure and wanted to come clean and tell her about her life, her biological mother, how it had made Kate such an overprotective parent, and how many times he wanted to bring it up as she got older. He was always overruled. What he did not want to discuss with her and felt it better that she forget was her kidnapping. It sounded as if someone either had her drive or drove her to Las Vegas for unknown reasons, and that person knows what really happened to her. The doctor examined her and there weren't signs of rape or STDs. Hearing all this, Mike recognized Ella to have a special brain that knew just how much emotional turmoil she could handle. He would go forward with the story that she had been in an accident and mugged. They would have her in her own bed by tomorrow.

The doctor came in a few minutes later with two pills for her to take. Janie remembered his discussion of the yellow-orange pill used for post-traumatic stress patients. She was unsure of the other one. As he handed them to her along with a glass of water, he explained these would relieve some of the pain and also help with her internal injuries. Janie realized she may be spitting out antibiotics for her gunshot wound but wanted nothing to do with their drugs. She would take only what she got over the counter for pain. In an effort to distract Dr. Colter, who seemed uncomfortable, she asked him for some Sprite instead as she felt a little nauseous. She held the two pills between her palm and closed pinky finger and looked as if she put them in her mouth to swallow like most patients would. Before he got her a Sprite, Dr. Colter watched her "take" the pills.

Upon his return, Janie was trying to get out of the bed to use the restroom. He helped her by unhooking some of the machines and the IV.

"I don't think you will need these anymore. Unfortunately, I need to give you a tetanus shot and then a final checkup before you can be on your way," he said, trying to sound convincing.

"Thanks, Doctor. I hope I wasn't too much trouble." Janie wanted to say so much more, but she saw fear in his eyes.

She was certain he did not want to know anything more and wanted her to stay in her current supposed state of mind. He nodded and left the room so she could have privacy. As soon as she was in the restroom, she realized how much she really had to pee. She also flushed the pills down the toilet and felt a little less queasy. Weakly, she made it back to the bed. Her leg was throbbing.

"Dammit, she thought, maybe the other pill was to help with the pain.

Well, she'd rather deal with pain than lose her mind. Janie wondered just how much they had told her father. She knew he'd do what he thought best for her, so they must've concocted a huge lie. She was glad he was here, in any case. At least she could be sure that someone would be watching them. Just as she was feeling the tiniest bit secure that she had played her part well, Dr. Colter came in to give her a once over and a "tetanus" shot before releasing her home.

The last thing she remembered before passing out was the needle in her arm and the doctor wishing her the best of luck. His face was a blur within seconds. Now, all she could do was dream about Chase and what they might have had. There wasn't even time to grieve, but there would be plenty of time for that later.

Chapter 34

DESERT RAIN

F rom Chase's position crouching behind the large boulder, he
heard his beloved Jeep explode into thousands of pieces and
saw the sky just above the canyon light up in shades of orange
with gray smoke snaking through. The two stocky men swerved and
braked too quickly in the sand, almost barreling over the edge. They
jumped out of the car just in time to see Chase's Jeep blow and light
up the canyon. Chase hoped they would believe him to be dead. He
figured there was a damn good chance of their thinking in that direction as they nearly went over themselves in the darkness.

He was close, real close. In fact, he heard one yell to the other,
"Jesus Christ! That could have been us! I'm not going to worry about
checking his vitals, Ronny. One down, right?"

"I ain't goin' down there, man. If he's not dead then he walks
on water. Let's get out of here before anyone shows up. Be careful
when you back out. Actually, I want to check something up ahead
near the road. Once you turn around, I'll hop in. Good luck," he
said, half laughing. Chase could hear his voice was a little freaked

out after the near-death miss.

At first, they drove away carefully, then when they met the road, they were at full throttle. Chase had one thought in mind: Janie. He needed to see if they had all taken the bait before contacting Billy. He had consciously put his cell phone in his pocket. He had been around long enough in too many situations to count where it saved his life. It had not fallen out. He was a lucky guy. Just not completely and not today.

Right away, he called Billy. He answered out of breath, "Chase, my God, it's you! Where the hell are you? I'll pick you up. We need to have a talk."

"Billy, did you get back to Janie? Is she safe?" He said every word clearly so Billy would answer him directly.

"Chase, I made it to one of the many warehouses Johnny has around the city and lost them. I changed cars and headed back up to the old building where Janie was in the car. As I drove up on the hill, I saw an ambulance at the scene along with a police car. Chase, I waited to see how she was doing so I could follow them to the hospital and make sure she'd be okay. I . . . I . . . shit, Chase," he said as his voice cracked. "I did not get the chance to follow them. The EMT shook his head. The last thing I saw him do was put a sheet over her head while putting her body in the back of the ambulance. The bastards must've shot her randomly in too many of the wrong places. I'm so sorry. I know how you felt about her." His voice trailed off in a whisper, "I waited so long to meet her."

Chase could not answer for a few long seconds. They both sat on the phone quietly as Chase finally sighed and said, "So did I, Billy. I waited my whole life to meet her and now she's gone."

"Chase, let me pick you up and we'll figure this out together. We need to find out who is behind this."

Chase hung up silently and walked over to the cliff. He threw his phone in with the car. He needed to disappear. At this moment, he could not think, but he knew where to go—a place no one knew about. Well, not many people. He walked to the nearest gas station, found an unoccupied four-wheel-drive SUV and drove through the dark, peaceful desert. He was numb. He kept thinking, *Who could have done this?* He knew this desert like the back of his hand. Chase made it to his Airstream in an hour and a half. Once inside, the place looked disheveled from his rushed state to grab all of the items Janie and he would need to camp out in Red Rock on their way to Vegas. In the corner of his couch, he saw her vintage Rolling Stones T-shirt and bandana, the clothes she'd had on the day they met. He pulled them up to his face, closed his eyes, and tried to breathe in her scent. He could not imagine her dead.

His thoughts went back to that first day—her cut forehead and the beat-up car, which clearly she had driven after wrecking it. And her smile . . . She lit up the desert in the morning. He had to admit, he never would have stopped if it hadn't been for her dynamic smile. Her terrible predicament did not seem to faze her. In fact, she seemed playful and rather happy, for a stranded soul. This is what took him off guard at first and what made him fall in love with her so quickly. She never disclosed what had happened or, in fact, if she was running from anyone. At that moment, Chase made the decision to get her MG early in the morning and see what he could find out about Janie. He may have been blinded but had never let any woman allow him to feel so intensely.

Deciding to stay the night in peace and get some rest, Chase built a small fire outside the trailer. He looked up to see clouds filtering through the stars, carefully weaving in and around each tiny dot of light. As he remembered Janie's sarcasm as she dodged his "constellation moves" and somewhat cliché lines, a thought occurred to him. Janie seemed to be looking for something else in the sky that evening. She was preoccupied with her own dilemma. That was part of her charm, Chase thought. He detected an air of grace, mystery, and intelligence about her. As he wondered about Janie's uncanny ability of smiling right through you yet into your very soul, Chase could not stop feeling that he missed some glaring sign right in front of him. He made a decision not to grieve just yet. He was not going to believe she was dead. How could someone so beautiful, intelligent, and spontaneous not be sorely missed? Perhaps someone had been chasing her all along. Maybe she was working with the wrong people from the beginning. He'd had a feeling earlier that she may have been running from someone or something but had let it go so he could focus on the moment. Too many things were happening with work to worry about the thoughts she had been keeping to herself. At that very moment, rain started to fall from the sky in sheets. The stars were no longer visible and Chase's fire made a sizzling sound as smoke rose. Quickly, he went inside the trailer. Instead of staying the night, Chase headed toward Joe's garage where they left Janie's car. He wanted to investigate while it was still dark.

The Hummer he had stolen would be missed, for sure, yet it didn't hold a candle to his Jeep. He'd need to ditch this car somewhere and find another soon. On his drive over to the run-down gas station, Chase began thinking about what he might find of interest in her car. People left so many personal things in their cars, not to mention the registration information. Also, he needed to trust Billy and Blake. Another conversation was needed with Billy about exactly what he saw the other night behind the theater building. The connections Blake had used to get Chase out of the area were invaluable. As he drove into the station in darkness, Chase saw large dents in the dirt where puddles had collected from the evening's rain. He drove the car around to where Janie's MG had been, but it was gone. In the back of his mind, he had worried this might be the case. This was the only lead he could think of regarding Janie Blue. Even her name was evasive. It might as well be Jane Doe.

Now, he would drive to the Pioneer Bar in hopes Blake would be closing up. Drawing near it, Chase parked behind the mock ghost town hotel and walked to the back entrance. It was about 3 a.m., yet Chase saw a light on in the back room where Blake would stay when he had a particularly late night or a few drinks himself. He did not want to barge in as Blake would surely be jumpy tonight after talking to Billy. At the same time, he wanted to avoid any other intruders that may be there instead of Blake. He decided to wait and watch until he saw Blake's large shadow walking casually toward the hall. Chase knocked seven times softly. This was always a running joke with them. A secret knock could get too complicated, so he would knock seven times, wait, and then softly try it seven more times. Just after the seventh knock, Blake opened the door with a sad smile on his face and pulled Chase inside.

"Man, you had Billy and me worried. What in the hell did you do with your phone after you two talked? We had no way to find you and help you out."

"I know. I threw it in the canyon like a fucking idiot. I briefly thought I could do this on my own. Since I have no idea who put this hit on me, I really need your help getting out of here. Before I disappear, Billy and I need to talk. Any idea as to his whereabouts?"

Out of the dark hallway, Billy appeared. He looked tired and defeated but walked toward Chase and grasped his shoulders and shook his head. They did not need to say anything. Sadness penetrated the room. However, Chase was not giving up just yet. That was not his style nor did he believe all hope was lost.

Chapter 35

LOOKS ARE DECEIVING

"**B**illy, did you think it was a little strange that an ambulance was there so quickly? Believe me, my sense of time was out of whack after driving toward Red Rock and watching my car sail over the cliff. Those two guys who were after me were idiots, but I needed them to tell their boss or bosses that I was dead rather than ambush them and send them after my Jeep. They could not have been Global Insurance's team, nor do I have any feeling that they were O'Shea's. Therefore, I am asking you if anything seemed funny about the guy in the ambulance. You said there was only one, right? And one police officer?"

"Yeah, well, I didn't look to see if anyone was in the driver's seat, but now that you mention it, why would they not all be out helping or talking? No cop goes to a scene like that without a partner, and any ambulance has at least two people to assist. Hmm, what are you thinking, Chase?"

Chase thought for a moment and shrugged his shoulders, saying, "I am trying to figure out if this had anything to do with Janie. I also want to believe that she may be alive. Let's work on finding out where she was living and if she had any bad skeletons in the closet. I mean, Jesus, Billy, look at what happened when she was a kid. You said you looked for her for years and came up empty. And, this is *you* looking for her, not just anyone. Someone had to have some clout to pull this off."

"First of all, idiots or not, they found you and almost killed you, Chase. Let's get you out of here for a bit. Secondly, your theory is interesting, but you really don't know if this is connected to Global. They would have every reason to be pissed off if they knew you led them astray. I'll work on Janie's whereabouts again. I haven't searched for her in years and things may have changed. Paperwork might be released now or maybe someone can be paid off. It really was a dead end, but now that I know she may be alive, I will do everything I can. Blake, get Chase over to Manny's. He'll find a place for you to go until I see where this hit came from, Chase."

Blake got on the phone right away and reached in his closet while talking. Chase was taken aback for a minute as his guard had been down. In all seriousness, Blake looked at Chase and then handed him a new cell phone. He laughed at Chase's suspicious expression.

"Really, Chase, relax for five, okay? Here is your lifeline. I have my number and Billy's in here, plus an alternative as a last resort in case you can't get in touch with us in an emergency. Let's get going while it's still dark. Hey, how did you get here?"

"Oh, well, I left you a nice Hummer behind the old hotel to figure out. An added bonus. It's pretty nice—I am sure someone would like it back. It's yours now."

"Thanks, Chase. I'll have it put in the warehouse before the sun rises."

After an hour of driving, they made it to a small house near Lake Mead. It looked inconspicuous, blending in perfectly with the many vacation homes. Blake pulled up and the garage door opened on cue. They drove into the garage. As Chase opened the door, he was met by a guy who looked to be about twenty introducing himself as Manny. He was a lot younger than Chase expected. Actually, he looked like a punk kid who might be stealing cars for a living. His hair was slicked back, and he wore torn blue jeans and a faded black T-shirt.

Manny was respectful, shaking Chase's hand and saying, "I have a perfect plan for you, Chase. No worries."

Blake looked at Chase reassuringly. "Manny is the best we have when it comes to disappearing. You can trust him," he said as he patted him on the back.

Blake left him with the understanding that he would continue working with Billy and hopefully more of O'Shea's guys to find out just who put out this hit. At the same time, he and Billy would dive into a hardcore search for Janie. Blake wasn't convinced she was alive but hoped so for his friends' sake. Besides, she would be nice to see again. He genuinely liked Janie. That was rare for Blake to say.

After Blake left, Manny led Chase through the kitchen to what looked like a butler's pantry. Chase thought this seemed pretty fancy for a young guy living alone. He was hungry, though, come to think of it.

"So, Manny, you gonna make us some bacon and eggs?" he said with a laugh.

Manny gave him a grin. "Wait 'til you see this one, Chase."

He pushed the buttons almost in a code on the refrigerator ice-maker. Chase saw him punch in light, crushed, water, and light again. What the hell was he doing, he thought. A green light appeared on the ice button, and Manny pulled the door open. Chase was definitely impressed. It opened up to a room full of computers and screens and looked like the inside of a casino security room.

"Not many people get to see this, Chase. You must be in the circle. I am kind of the technology guru for Billy. I like it here, and I like being alone. I will get you a passport. Billy thinks you need to be out of the country. I can safely get you to Thailand, Mexico, or Costa Rica, okay? So, where would you like to be tomorrow evening?"

"I'll take you up on Costa Rica. If I'm there for a while I'd like to check out the rain forest."

"Fine. You'll have a great boat ride down. Now, I know you were hoping there was some food in the refrigerator. Help yourself to the one in here. It's always stocked with fruits, veggies, cheese, and crackers. I know, I'm kind of a health nut, but I never wanted to turn into one of those fat computer geeks with bad skin. There is also beer and OJ. Here's a paper. This is going to take some time."

Chase thought he was a quirky but nice, trustworthy kid with a lot of knowledge. Pretty much a genius, in his mind. He wondered how Billy found him.

He responded, "No problem, Manny, take your time. I'll help myself."

As he grabbed something to eat, he eyed a cot in the corner and decided to get a little shut-eye. His thoughts drifted toward the day and night before this nightmare happened. Down to his core he felt that Janie was in trouble—but still alive.

Chapter 36

POSITIVE ATTITUDE

Resuming her old life was complicated. Everything had turned upside down and had her head spinning as if she'd been on five high-impact roller coasters in a row. Ella now felt closer to Janie and the uninhibited side of her personality. Until recently, she had not known she had it in her. Acting as if nothing had changed was necessary for her own safety and possibly her father's. She had already indirectly killed Chase by her actions and now fully understood the power of politics and the price paid when interfering in the high-stakes game.

She was getting ready to attend her mother's memorial service near her father's house on the island. Focusing on the preparations dulled the pain she was dealing with each day. Her feelings for her mother ran so deeply, as did the sea of emotions within their complex relationship. At the same time, she could not stop grieving for her biological mother, Eliza Jane. The memories that flooded back with such unexpected intensity shoved her back in time as if it had happened yesterday.

She felt conflicted thinking about both their untimely deaths. Of course, the pain she tried to push away the furthest was that of losing Chase. She had known him for such a short time but had never known the meaning of perfect chemistry nor exposed herself to such vulnerability. Perhaps it was because he did not ask much from her and let her be exactly herself. It may have been selfish, but she knew he accepted her for who she was, and, somehow, he touched her very soul. If there was such a thing as soul mates, she understood the meaning now. Unfortunately, she would never really know what might have been. If only she could put that memory away while she tried in vain to be the Ella everyone had always known. Thankfully, her many small breakdowns and her tear-filled eyes could be attributed to her mother's death by everyone around her.

She took a deep breath and prepared to walk into the room where her father and Dan patiently awaited. In her navy-blue Chanel knit suit, Ella made her entrance with a forced smile on her face. Her hair was pinned halfway up and the rest hung in manicured, smooth waves. She had bronzer on but felt unusually pale. Suddenly having the urge to vomit, she looked up and excused herself. She ran to the restroom. Her nerves really had gotten the best of her. Dan waited for her outside the bathroom.

"Ella, honey, you okay in there? There is a car waiting to take us to the memorial."

She couldn't stand listening to his fake concern but could only act graciously in return. As she threw water on her face, the bile still left its mark on her throat. She rinsed her mouth out with a small hotel-size bottle of mouthwash from the medicine cabinet. Thank God her mother kept all of those. She always made sure that they never left the shampoos, lotions, or any other complimentary "goodies" from hotels they stayed in. Now she knew where they were kept. The guests had a choice of an array of tiny bottles to sample when staying at her parents' home.

Opening the door into Dan's face made her stand up straight

and blink her eyes. She tried to act without fear or anger, so she looked down and walked toward the front of the house where the car was waiting. He took her arm and walked alongside her as though it were his political duty.

"Dan, really, I'm fine. Just a bug, I think, mixed with a lot of emotions. Do you know where I can find my father?"

He pointed to the car. "He's waiting inside the car. I told him to give us a minute."

"I'll be fine in the car. I grabbed a plastic bag just in case but certainly hope I don't need to use it."

He noticed how sad and vulnerable she seemed. He liked that. It made him feel that she needed him. After they told her about the mugging and the accident, she seemed like a frightened child in need of protection. As long as she could keep up the image of a highly capable future senator's wife, then he liked this new side of her. In fact, he was trying to charm her. He was impatient about the thought of giving her time to heal from her bruises and wounds as well as get through her mother's funeral before he attempted to get her into bed again.

When he touched her, she seemed to go cold but would smile tentatively, saying, "Dan, I just need some time to feel like myself again."

The doctor told him to back off until she'd had at least three weeks of the pills he gave her. So far, Ella's memory seemed blocked from the time of the car accident. After discussing more with her dad and a trusted psychologist, every indicating factor led him to believe she would not remember. It seemed indicative of her reaction to her biological mother's murder. He was glad everything worked out as planned. His wife was truly a great package for his career, not to mention a new challenge for him. She had never been crazy in bed yet always a willing, dutiful wife, never denying him. Now, he wanted her physically more than ever and she was unavailable. For now . . .

Sitting next to her father throughout the service was very comforting for Ella. He put his hand on hers and wiped away her streaming tears with a handkerchief. He was old- fashioned in that way and always carried one. Dan looked uncomfortable and very serious. He placed his hand on her knee, leaving a stinging feeling through her skin. She wanted to throw it off of her but knew better. This was going to be a game of patience until she could find a way to prove what he had done. It could be a long time, she realized. She had a lot of time but was unsure of how she would be tested. During the service, Ella felt her stomach churning. She had some Altoid mints in her pocket. Discreetly, she popped two into her mouth, hoping to calm her nerves or trick her stomach.

Her face was pale as a ghost and she felt slightly dizzy. It took all of her emotional and physical strength to speak sweetly with all of her mother's friends, family, and mourners. By the time she got home, she went straight to her room to bed. Dan came in to give her some pills. One was probably a sedative. She thanked him and told him she just needed to sleep, but promised to take the pills before lying down.

Trying to sound appreciative and submissive, she said, "Dan, thanks for all of your help today. I really need to get some rest but will hope for a more positive outlook tomorrow. How do the polls look?"

He thought it pretty impressive that she thought of him right now, and he was ecstatic about the polls. There was news of them going to the memorial service for her mother and pictures taken of him looking like a supportive husband. He knew they looked like a great couple. Funerals, weddings, and births gave people in his position extra press time, which usually jacked up the numbers.

He pretended not to care about the polls and answered, "I haven't checked, but not to worry. I'll see you in the morning. Let me get you a glass of water to take those."

He went to the bathroom to get it for her. After handing her the glass, he kissed her forehead and quietly left the room, closing the door behind him. Ella waited a few minutes before getting up and flushing the pills down the toilet. She changed into her cozy cotton pajamas, took off her makeup, and fell into her soft bed. She was thankful that Dan had said he would see her in the morning. She did not need to worry about him sleeping next to her. That meant he was probably going to his longtime mistress for some attention. He was overdue, as he'd been playing the role of concerned husband for the past three weeks. He had been careful not to attempt having sex with Ella or put any pressure of that kind onto her thus far. She knew the time would come soon, though, as her wounds and bruises were now healed and her mother's service was over. His eyes were boring down on her more than ever, giving her subtle sexual looks and smiles she'd never seen before. She needed to prepare herself. She could not imagine sleeping with a murderer, but she was also realistic in how best to protect herself or those she loved until she could gather more information. Surprisingly, sleep came easily for her tonight.

Chapter 37

ALLIANCES

When he was certain Ella had fallen asleep, Dan grabbed his gym bag and texted Marco to drive behind the house to pick him up so they could talk. He told him not to worry. He gave her something that would knock her out until morning. Marco wondered if she'd be okay alone in the house. He offered to stay in case she woke up and an impromptu excuse was necessary for Dan's whereabouts.

"Marco, I think she really will sleep the night away just fine, but if you are worried, stay in the guest room downstairs. I, on the other hand, am going to have hot, not-so-nice sex with my not-so-sweet girlfriend. I have really been good lately playing the perfect husband, and this is a fantastic opportunity. Drive around the back, as usual."

After dropping him off, Marco decided to make sure the mix of pills had not affected Ella strangely. She would not be happy waking in a panic and finding out her husband was out in the middle of the night. Marco had become quite good at making up plausible excuses. In any case, he liked Ella. She was incredibly beautiful, very smart, and pretty funny when she lightened up. He felt terrible for what could have happened to her, but he had done his best to prevent it. Luckily, he had prevailed. He thought Dan was an idiot. In reality, Marco's main purpose these days was to keep him in line until he was elected senator. After that, he'd see what his chances were for higher political aspirations. Each rung on the ladder Dan took gave Marco more clout with the higher-ups in his organization.

When Ella woke up, she knew Dan would be gone. This was a chance to see if anything new of interest would pop up on his desk. It could be a name, a phone bill, or a new appointment in his calendar, which could give her some vital information. As she walked downstairs toward the office in her pajamas and robe with her hair piled on her head, her thoughts were focused on betraying Dan to the fullest. So intent was she in her thoughts that she did not even notice Marco in the kitchen making coffee. Luckily, he decided to make himself known to her as he did not want to frighten her.

"Uh . . . Ella . . . are you up? It's Marco."

Thank God, she thought. She was just about to go into Dan's private office. Now what? Was she being watched twenty-four seven?

"Marco, good morning. What are you doing here? Dan must have left early and told you to check on me," she said, nicely giving him the excuse as she did not want to watch him backpedal.

"Sorry to bother you, Ella. Coffee is on. Just wanted to make sure you were up and okay. Dan said he gave you a sleeping aid and coupled with your day . . . Anyway, he had to be at work early for an important meeting and asked me to check in," he said with an air of admiration in his voice.

He also looked at her a bit more than he should have. He thought she looked great in the morning without makeup. He didn't usually see her like this, so casual. Actually, she did look rested considering, and he knew he should be on his way.

"Sorry again about your mother. I understand it was a nice service, Ella. You have a good day."

She smiled carefully and thanked him for checking in. As she shut the door softly, Ella turned the lock and put her back to the door once inside. Slowly, she sank to the floor feeling sick, exhausted, and afraid. Marco was the guy who ordered the hit on Chase. She knew he probably saved her life as he did not make rash decisions. He was the one who talked Dan into waiting until she came to, telling Dan that he thought she did not remember anything. He gave her the idea to plead amnesia. She must have it in her to lock away things like she did as a child, so why not this? She would do her best to pretend. At the moment, she needed to find a toilet, sink, or bowl. Steadying herself, she walked back upstairs to bed. Later on, Dan called to say he'd be coming home late and not to bother with dinner.

From the time she woke up the following morning, Ella felt sick as a dog. The master bathroom toilet was being put to the test as she could not keep anything down. Now, she thought either she was being poisoned or there was a small chance she could be pregnant. Either way, she was in a compromised position. A plan was needed and fast. Ella's neglected best girlfriend, Stacey, was also a pediatrician in the city. She would need to be discreet. Thoughts of running to the drugstore or grocery store for a pregnancy test were unthinkable. First of all, she was probably being watched by Marco, the press, or even nosy neighbors or acquaintances. She knew exactly what to do. She picked up the phone and dialed Stacey at her office.

A soft-spoken woman's voice answered, "Lincoln Plaza Medical, may I help you?"

"Yes, may I speak with Dr. Rollings, please? Could you tell her it's Ella?"

Stacey answered right away, "Hey, sweetie, how you doing? I am in between patients for two minutes. What's on your mind? Everything okay?"

Chapter 38

FRIEND IN NEED

Ella laughed under her breath as her busy friend always bombarded her with questions to which she never had time to hear the answers. Ella replied, "I just miss my friend and am having a rough day after the memorial. I know you're superbusy, Stace, but do you have time this afternoon for a quick coffee or tea?" She knew her friend would make time if she could.

"Absolutely, El, how's one o'clock? Can we meet at the outdoor cart by my office? It's a beautiful day. Thank God for summers in Seattle, right? I need as much sun as possible. Are we on?"

"That sounds perfect, thanks. I'll see you at one sharp as I know your crazy schedule."

Ella needed to get some crackers and ginger ale in her body pronto. She'd be dehydrated by lunch at this rate.

Managing to take a hot shower and get dressed was impressive, considering her state. The crackers and ginger ale helped tremendously. Perhaps having a reason to get out of the house on a sunny day helped as well. Ella threw on a pair of soft, thin jeans and a racerback tank as she grabbed her navy windbreaker, not knowing what the weather in Washington would bring. She decided to forget the sunscreen, needing every bit of vitamin D and the potential for a light tan to liven up her pale face. She longed to feel the hot sun of Vegas and wished to relive the drive in the Jeep with Chase.

From her house, it was only a fifteen-minute drive and a quick ferry ride to Seattle without traffic. Thankfully, she was not at her father's house on the island. She'd never make it across on that ferry in her condition. The short time in the car gave her a moment to think about what to say to Stacey. She had always been able to tell her everything. Never once had Stacey broken her trust. She was a solid, loyal friend. By the time she parked the car, Ella knew her friend could help out.

Seeing Stacey at the kiosk as she arrived with five minutes to spare, Ella felt very grateful to have her as a friend. She had a sudden urge to cry for that reason alone, but held back the flood of tears.

Stacey waved happily and came bouncing over to Ella. She was five-three and voluptuous—a far cry from the scrawny eight-year-old Ella had met at the park when they were kids. She had shiny, long blond hair, fair skin, and huge brown eyes. Stacey had a beaming smile and a personality that would make even a forlorn child with chicken pox grin back. She had chosen the perfect profession.

After grabbing her friend in a hearty hug, Stacey stood back with Ella's hands in hers and simply stated, "You're still gorgeous, but you definitely need some sunshine and a pick-me-up. Seriously, El, you are going through a really sad time right now, but I see a bright spot in your future," she added in a mystical yet mocking tone.

Ella looked at her friend with tears in her eyes and said, "As my best friend, you promise not to judge me, ever—right?"

"Of course, goes with the territory. God knows you could have judged me over and over during our friendship, but you never failed me. Why are you asking me this?"

In all seriousness and with a soft voice, Ella told her friend,

"Stace, I think I could be pregnant, but not by Dan. I need your help. If I am not, then I still need your help. There are a few things happening in my life that I cannot keep locked in or I'll just burst!" With a seriously strained face, Ella tried to hold back the tears, yet they streamed down her cheeks anyway.

Stacey did not act shocked. She felt strongly that Ella expected her friend's "doctor" personality right now.

With that in mind, she calmly stated, "Let's just march back into my office like you're walking me back. I'll pass you a little test like we used to pass secret notes in class, okay? Remember how good we were at that?"

She made Ella smile slightly. They looped arms and made their way to Stacey's private office. As they were walking back, Stacey texted her receptionist to cancel or send all her appointments to her partner unless they were urgent. Once inside her office, Stacey handed Ella a test stick and told her she'd need only one.

"If it shows a plus sign, we need to have a much more detailed conversation, right?"

Closing the bathroom door, Ella felt that this was such a weird concept. She peed on the stick and stared at it. Certainly, she did not expect to see a plus sign appear so quickly. She waited for the full minute in case it changed to a negative, but it did not. Part of her was elated. There was no question in her mind that this was Chase's baby. In all the years they'd been together and with all of the "accidents," she and Dan had not conceived. Also, she hadn't had sex with him for a few weeks before her car accident. On the brighter side, at least she had not been poisoned.

Chapter 39

ART OF DECEPTION

The gravity of the situation grounded Ella as she closed her eyes for a brief moment and imagined lying next to Chase. She felt a sense of peace knowing that a part of him would always be with her. Now, she needed to leave the quiet bathroom and talk to her very patient friend. Telling her without most of the details would be difficult, but it must be done.

As she came through the door, Stacey tried smiling tentatively and broke the ice with, "I guess I know the answer already, hon. You've been in there a while."

Stacey was taken aback by her friend's statue-like, peaceful trance. Ella looked to her like a different person. She seemed strong and calm. The Ella she knew would have fallen apart by now.

It had been over ten grueling minutes that Stacey practically had to tape her own mouth shut and sit on her hands so that she wouldn't rip the door open or call out to Ella. She knew Ella needed time, and Stacey truly wanted to be there for her friend. She stepped out of her doctor image and went to her friend, giving her a great big hug. She sat with Ella on the couch while she cried and even giggled at one time. Finally, Ella told her what had transpired the past four weeks, leaving out a few major details. She did not say that Dan was a murderer nor did she talk about the "incident" where she almost died. Her story ended in an entirely different way.

She said, "I came to my senses after he was suddenly gone the morning after we had amazing sex and decided to come home. Really, that's all she wrote, Stacey."

As difficult as it was to describe Chase in such a cold way, she was not lying to Stacey. He was gone, just in a very different way.

After Stacey questioned her, Ella said, "Dan was, of course, worried sick about me and his publicity ratings, but he allowed me my much-needed space. He thought I had gone off the deep end after Mom's death and just needed a few days in a hotel alone. He was thankful that my father never sent out the troops and detectives. Thank goodness Dad did not make a scene, or he would have jeopardized Dan's precious career."

"Just one thing, Ella. How did you drive home? I thought your car was almost totaled." Stacey could tell her friend was lying. They'd known each other for too long. Ella always bit her bottom lip.

Ella was determined not to involve her friend any more than need be. However, she was not thinking so quick on her feet lately, and really did not know how far she could be pushed before breaking. Ella opened her mouth to cover up her lie with another absurd lie, but knew her friend had already seen the expression of utter despair on her face.

"Dammit, Ella. I do not care what you've done. I am your friend and you look like you need one right now. Tell me everything. I am very good at lying, but you are pathetic! I'll help you get through this; I promise. Spill it!"

She started with the accident and her strange dreams. Next, she described how she felt like a completely different person for a while without a thought of what had happened moments, days, weeks, or years before the accident. Kind of like a renewed soul or something.

"Stace, maybe that is what it's like when we die. The feeling was liberating. Also, my feelings were so strong to drive to Las Vegas. It was as if I were being compelled in some weird way. Seriously, I just went with it. I can't even remember stopping for gas. In fact, I drove that damn old MG until it quit. That is where I met Chase. At that point, everything became very vivid."

"All right, my friend, let's put aside the seriousness of this situation for a minute. How hot was this maverick man of yours?"

"Almost too good to be true. He was witty, brutally honest, and a perfect gentleman—well, for the most part," she said, laughing and not realizing the tears were streaming down her face. "We had three amazing days and nights. I think he knew what I wanted more than anyone, yet he asked for nothing. I know it sounds crazy, Stace, but there was a soul mate kind of connection there."

"Right, Ella, but here he had this gorgeous woman feeling liberated and totally at ease with herself. Is that how you'd describe yourself on a typical day? I mean, what the hell kind of reality is that?" she asked Ella with both sarcasm and concern.

"Listen, Stacey," she said pleadingly, "the next part of the story gets so intense you may wish we had left things like they were before. I am in a lot of trouble right now, but not with the law. Someone is after me, but this is not simple and I cannot involve the police at the moment. Are you still sure you want to know more? I am not worried about your loyalty, but your safety."

Without hesitation, Stacey sighed and said, "Yes, hon, I'll help you with this. Besides, if it is as bad as you're warning, then you cannot possibly take this on alone."

Ella wanted to laugh and cry at the same time as she felt her throat tightening at the thought of talking about this very situation.

After swallowing the lump in her throat, Ella came to the point, quickly saying, "He had Chase killed, Stacey. Dan did. He put a hit out on him to save his political career. I am quite sure he would've asked the same fate of me except the doctor was sure I had PTSD amnesia and also thought I'd been kidnapped. Marco—Dan's right-hand man—Dan, and the good doctor decided to give me certain meds of which you are probably well aware to continue my memory loss of the traumatic event. Dan was pretty convinced all would work, and I'd be his ticket to the Senate playing the unwavering hostess and politician's wife."

"Okay, back up, Ella. Were you at the scene where Chase was killed?" Her friend was aghast and had turned flushed with anger.

As hard as it was to put herself back in time to the day Chase died, Ella did so for Stacey. She owed her the story in its entirety as bits and pieces would leave Stacey frustrated and ready to call the FBI or the police. She explained everything from the woman in her dreams being her biological mother and how she was knocked out. At the time, Ella was overwhelmed with emotions regarding her mother's death and Billy to realize the severity of Billy's words to Chase. She did not care about a hit on him, and really did not know why someone would be after him anyway.

"Stacey, it was a whirlwind. Chase knocked me out for my own safety and to get out of there fast. Until that calculated blow to my head, I had forgotten about my life at home almost entirely. Imagine my surprise waking up to hear Dan and Marco discussing Chase's death and deciding my fate. Amnesia was the only way out. That coupled with the fact that I overheard them saying I may have been kidnapped since someone saw me get punched and put in the car with my hands bound."

Trying to process everything quickly, Stacey had a few more pertinent questions. "So, you're saying that this guy with Chase, Billy, killed your biological mother? How old were you, and why don't you remember?"

Amazed at the relief she was feeling but understanding Stacey's confusion, she nodded her head and proceeded with the story. "Yes, he did. I am still trying to figure out the part about why I can't remember or how I was adopted by my father and Kate . . . I mean my mother. This really upsets me, but I can only come up with amnesia again as it really did happen to me after the accident. Literally, Stace, I didn't really know who I was but did not care. I was numb, yet felt so intensely. It felt wonderful at the time."

"Ella, I know you are kind of manic right now and this is almost too much information for me to process, so let's just dissect this a little at a time and figure things out, okay?" she said slowly to her friend as she would to one of her grief-stricken patients in pediatrics.

Admitting that her life was a mess, Ella squeezed her eyes shut before speaking again. When she opened her eyes, tears started flowing uncontrollably. Stacey went to her friend and put her arms around her tightly. They sat on the couch as Ella cried for five straight minutes.

"This baby is giving me hope, Stacey. I have something more to protect than just myself. In order to be free of Dan and be safe, I need to concoct a plan to retrieve enough information and documentation of what he has done to put him in jail forever. More importantly, I need the information to get into the hands of Chase's friend. Right now, I am not sure which one I am more afraid of: Dan or Billy. They are both killers. This is why I have not gone to see him. Also, I believe I am being watched even as we speak. I'll need to come up with a great excuse as to why you and I spent the afternoon in your office. Maybe I'll say you were having a crisis with your love life. That'll creep him out and shut him up. You know what a homophobe he is!" Ella laughed for the first time all day. "So, do you understand why I think calling the police in would be a terrible plan?"

"Yes, I believe I do. They would twist the story around. Especially since your mother died, you'd been in an accident, and now you are pregnant. Speaking of, you will need to make sure Dan believes this is his baby you are carrying. Do you have a plan for that?"

"I know he is attracted to me, Stacey, and I've been untouchable for the past four weeks. I . . . uh . . ." She looked hesitant.

"If you can't do this, Ella, we'll figure something else out. I'm still not so sure that getting the right authorities involved is a bad idea. I always knew that guy was an ass, but never knew he had enough guts to have someone killed. It makes me sick to think of you with such an unstable, diabolical idiot. More than that, I cannot imagine what someone like that would do if given more political power. It sounds like he has people helping him, wanting favors returned. Do you know who these people could be, Ella?"

"Not yet, but I've gone through some paperwork. Do you remember how I aced those tests?"

"Ah, yes, your photographic memory. You swore me to secrecy! How could I forget? I was sure it was magic, and you were some kind of sister to Samantha from *Bewitched*. If I told anyone, I'm pretty sure you made it known with a sarcastic laugh that I'd be struck by lightning. In the back of my mind, I was never quite sure . . ." She smiled at her friend's amazing talent and the memory of their childhood.

"Well, I'd really just forgotten about using it until recently. I've been trying to find a way to get into his locked office drawers undetected. I doubt he'd have proof, but perhaps numbers or names that could prove useful in the future."

"All right, Ella, try to focus on that little one growing, okay? One minute at a time. Remember not to bite your lip when you are lying. Also, take a couple of seconds before answering and don't rush your answers. You'll seem nonchalant and more at ease. Lastly, try to smile sweetly. No one can resist you when you smile," she said, then hugged her friend and tried to project good vibes and strength to her.

Chapter 40

A FORCED PLAN

Ella left the building and, sure enough, just as she was getting in the car, Dan called. Did someone already call him up to relay information on her whereabouts, or was she getting more paranoid, she wondered.

"Hi, Dan, how's your day going?" she answered sweetly.

Dan thought she sounded very calm and almost happy. He tread lightly by saying, "Just calling to see if we can have dinner out tonight. Are you feeling up to it?"

Setting her hand on her stomach, she responded, "It's been a while since we've been out, hasn't it, Dan? Can we go somewhere quiet? Maybe Chez Michele?"

Now, Dan was intrigued even more. She had not seemed a very cooperative partner since before her mother's death and after his last indiscretion. It was a good thing she did not know about the multitude of others. She had seen him pushing back a "friend's" hair and whispering into her ear in a corner at a party. He had had a little too much to drink and did not call her bluff that she knew about Carolyn, the cute blonde. She seemed so certain— as if she had proof—that he did not want to make the situation worse, and he caved. What an idiot he had been! It turned out she had known nothing. "Just a hunch," she'd told him later as she stormed off to her friend's house.

"Chez Michele sounds perfect. Can you be ready by seven? I'll come by right after my meeting and we'll leave from the house. I'm looking forward to seeing more of you this evening, Ella."

Well, it seemed she wasn't going to have to work too hard to persuade Dan. She was feeling a little less queasy today and took some valerian, an herbal aid to help her sleep. She wanted to feel up to the task, and knew she needed as much rest as possible right now.

Six fifteen came too quickly. She'd been exhausted after her day with Stacey and trying to plan her future. Focusing on one thing at a time would really help her get through the potential catastrophe ahead. Smoothly weaving around chaos would be her goal. As she opened her closet, Ella reached for a dress she had never worn, thinking it a little risqué. Now, it was the only dress in her closet she liked. Really, everything was ultraconservative and a bit matronly. Her desire to fit into the political world and become the kind of wife her mother thought she should be had pushed her in that direction. Slinking into the cool, silver, long tank dress made her feel sexy.

She slipped on silvery, gold-heeled shoes and could see the glint of the strappy tips just below the hemline. The dress was formfitting, so she selected a simple, long necklace and wrapped it around her slim neck three times. She decided to wear her hair up loosely and pull some waves around her face. Smoky eyes and nude lips created the demure look she was going for. As she pulled the pieces of hair out around her face, Ella thought of Chase and the night she was getting ready to meet him at the hotel bar. How different she felt that night—the butterflies were a far cry from the feeling of falling prey to a vicious snake.

She heard the door open at seven o'clock on the dot. Ella came into the foyer casually fastening her pearl earring and grabbing a matching cashmere shrug while Dan eyed her approvingly. He did not even want to go to the restaurant now that he saw her looking so chic and sexy, but he knew he needed to play a good game tonight.

"You look gorgeous, El. I've never seen you in that before," he added with a catlike smile.

Raising her eyebrow and smiling back as best she could, she thanked him and looped her arm through his.

"I'm famished, Dan. I hope they still have that great lobster bisque."

Food was not what he had in mind, but he'd enjoy looking at her. Dan knew how to charm a woman and he was up for the challenge now. He asked her about her day with Stacey.

Trying not to tense as she had already rehearsed this answer, she said it was kind of long as Stacey was going through a breakup with her latest flame and was a little heartbroken. She made sure not to bite her lip.

"Seriously, Dan, you know how some relationships get, right? As a guy, I am sure you can't even begin to imagine the drama of two women in a relationship," she teased.

"Uh . . . no . . . not particularly," he replied and quickly changed the subject. "So, how do you feel about the upcoming event for Project Hope next month? Do you think you're feeling up to tackling the cause?" He knew Ella loved working with the local children's homes and thought this might get her back into the swing of things.

"Yes. Absolutely. I need to jump back in and see positive changes happening. I know Mom would not want me to dwell." She thought they were at least having a decent conversation.

As the evening wore on, Dan brought up their honeymoon and fun times with friends. He kept refilling her wine, which she fed the lovely faux plant next to her every chance she could and sipped a bit so as not to create suspicions. She had never felt more focused. If she let her mind wander, it could end in a tearful disaster. Therefore, she decided to pretend she was an actor playing the role of a lifetime. At one point, she was sure she gave him her best Bette Davis eyes and Vivien Leigh flirtatious pout. Apparently, her efforts paid off as Dan did not even order dessert. He asked her if she'd mind taking hers to go.

He put his hand on her thigh during the car ride home and walked around to open the car door for her. Although he usually had good manners for the press, his were exceptional tonight. As they entered the house, Dan took her hand and led her silently upstairs to their bedroom. Dan wanted her more than ever before. She had definitely become a bit of a mystery and more of a challenge to him. The new look, the change in attitude, and even her mannerisms were subtle yet sultry. He wondered if she'd changed at all in bed. In fact, he was not going to waste any time waiting to find out. Before they were in the room, Dan took her sweater. His movements were unusually sly as he dropped it on the chair in the corner of the bedroom.

"I've missed you, Ella." He looked into her eyes, and she let him come to her.

Before he touched her, she slid out of the dress, turned and walked to the bed still in her heels. She knew this would make him crazy seeing her half-naked, smooth backside. It also gave her a chance to close her eyes and not glare at him. She had to change her mind-set away from the horrible things Dan had done, and try to remember him as a nice guy hopelessly interested in her when they first met. He didn't give her a chance to get to the bed. His pants and shoes were off faster than she could turn back around. It was like a switch went off.

As Dan had been drooling over her all night, he thought he'd test the water on her and change up their sex life. Also, he harbored a lot of pent-up anger, almost rage at the possibility that she had an affair with her "supposed" kidnapper. Something snapped. Dan put his palm to the small of her back and pushed her to the bed. As she stumbled nervously, she decided not to try to fight him or face him. If he wanted it this way, she'd play the game for one night. He liked the fear he felt from her and ripped off her silk thong. Without removing her bra, he grabbed her shoulder with one hand and right hip with the other. Swiftly and roughly, he shoved himself inside her over and over until he came. In his excitement, he didn't care or notice her pain. In fact, he actually whispered, "Stay down, bitch" at one point.

Afterward, he kissed her neck roughly and pulled her onto the bed. Ella was a little shocked and slightly numb. She was filled with hatred for this man who was looking down at her with full satisfaction on his face. She could tell he did not know what to say to her, nor was he ready to say anything. She carefully took off her heels and slid under the covers. Like Stacey said, she needed him to come inside her only one time. She realized that his actions gave her an excuse to be angry with him and avoid sex for a while until she could spring the news that she was pregnant. By that time, she would feign sickness and pregnancy as the culprit for her lack of sex drive. Ella hoped she would uncover some proof of what evil acts he had orchestrated and devise a plan to put him away as soon as possible.

Chapter 41

DOCTOR'S ORDERS

T he setting sun over the Pacific Ocean never gets monotonous, but it's a constant reminder of dreams unfulfilled. Chase watched the sun go down just until there was a faint hint of an orange curve above the deep blue sea. He spent his days hiking and checking out the hundreds of species of monkeys, birds, and snakes. Sometimes, he felt like a bad version of Indiana Jones, except nothing overly interesting ever really materialized. As he twisted his sun-streaked beard through his fingers, Chase decided it was time to move on. This really was not his style. He needed the vibrant city and was ready for society again. It had been two months since the tragedy in Las Vegas. By this time, everyone must have believed him dead and the interest in him was over. It was time to call Blake and get back to some semblance of reality. Chase hiked back to what he called the "tree house" in Drake Bay at the tip of Costa Rica on the outskirts of the rain forest. Upon his return, the bartender of the Tiki Hut handed him a mojito with extra ice, just the way he liked it.

"Carlos, can I get you to patch through a call for me?"

As he wiped the look of surprise off his face, Carlos said, "Sí, Chase. Anythin' for mi amigo."

This was the first time Chase had asked to make a call. Carlos figured he was dealing with a crisis as he was always deep in thought when he saw him from afar. He liked Chase and his witty American humor. Unlike a lot of the Americans, Chase listened to what the locals had to say and had great respect for his surroundings.

Back in Las Vegas, Dr. Colter was tucking his white shirt into blue jeans, getting ready for a much-needed reunion with his buddies from medical school. He tried to fluff his thinning hair with his hands, afraid to brush out any needed strands. He wanted to make a good impression tonight, as he had not seen some of these guys in years. Many of them were out in California, and a couple others stayed in Las Vegas. Tonight, they were going to check out the seven best hole-in-the-wall bars in the Vegas area. They would start out driving and decide on cabs later. As he headed out, Dr. Colter glanced at a picture of him and his friend Marco, back in Iraq. He turned the frame over. That story was over now. The favor he returned for Marco saving his life was really eating at him. He could not get that beautiful woman out of his mind. He hoped she was able to stick with the amnesia story and was smart enough to outwit Marco. In a last-minute effort, he had hinted to her that her story better stay straight, but he'd keep her secret. Dr. Colter was sickened by his hand in her "recovery," but glad it was him and not some quack who may have killed her either from his lack of medical knowledge or by saying too much. He needed this night and was definitely not the designated driver.

After three bars, Colter and the guys were pretty toasted. However, Dave, from San Diego, said they had to make it to this supposed haunted bar where all the Western film legends had gotten drunk in the past.

Dave tried his best John Wayne impersonation, saying, "Okay, Pilgrims, let's head on over to the last saloon, meet our posse, and drink some of that there whiskey or my name is not the Duke."

They all laughed and decided that for Dave's sake they'd hit one more bar for one more shot of whiskey. Colter definitely thought it was the best call as he stumbled in yelling, "A shot of whiskey for the house!" Since it was 2 a.m., they were the only ones in the bar. Well, the only ones except Blake, the bartender and manager.

Blake laughed at these white-collar clowns, but thought they looked pretty harmless and decided to let them have one drink. They cheered and sang "Walk the Line."

On their way out, he noticed one of them standing in place just staring at the phenomenal picture of Eliza Jane, Janie's mother, as she looked as if she were blowing a big kiss to all of the guests on their way out and beckoning them to come back again sometime.

The man stuttered, "I . . . I know that beautiful lady!"

Blake laughed and said, "We'd all like to know her, buddy. Say goodnight to her and be on your way."

Colter looked at the picture and in a silly gesture with his hand waved and called, "Goodnight, fair Janie, goodnight."

Chapter 42

LUCKY BREAK

B lake stopped in his tracks to make sure he heard correctly. Did this guy really know Janie? He hollered, "Hey, I ordered another round for all of you and a promised ride back to your hotel in a limo. I may even bring in the ladies from next door to amuse you."

Dave jumped at the chance to have another drink at this old ghost town bar, and the others went along. Blake called Carly and promised her he'd owe her one if she and a couple of the "show-girls" would entertain these fellas for fifteen minutes. She agreed, as always, to Blake's request. Luckily, they had not gotten ready for bed yet after their late shift and arrived within five minutes. They stayed at the small "haunted" hotel next door on late nights. While they flirted with the other guys, Blake made a beeline for Colter to try and casually ask him a few questions. At the same time, he asked for all their IDs, claiming it was to make sure none of them drove home. What he really wanted was Colter's information in case he needed to get in touch with him sooner than later.

"So, you know that pretty gal up there, eh? I don't even know where that picture came from," said Blake, "Must have been a party here that night."

"Well, I don't really know her," Colter whispered with a slur. "She was a very memorable patient I had a couple of months ago who feigned amnesia. I really hope she did have it."

"Wow, bet she was a hard one to let go home with a name like— what did you say her name was?"

"Ah, yes," he said, looking away with a drunken smile, "she told me Janie Blue, but then she said 'Ella,' realizing she had made a mistake. I told her I'd keep her secret. Not sure what kind of trouble she was in, but Marco seemed to like her, too, so I thought that a good sign. Don't know the other guy though. Kind of a jackass."

This was the first news anyone had heard that Janie could still be alive. None of their sources had turned up anything on her. It was like she vanished. It broke Billy's heart as he had lost track of her as a child and now this. Even the social workers and state came up with nothing. Her files were nonexistent even after all these years. Blake knew he couldn't do much more in front of these guys, so he wrote down his information and made sure the driver took everyone home first. Blake would meet him at the address from the license. First, he needed to call Billy.

Billy answered the phone annoyed. "Blake, it's 3 a.m. This better be good."

Chapter 43

MISTAKEN IDENTITY

"I may have found a link to Janie, Billy. She really may be alive. Meet me at this address outside in one hour and we'll find out more together from this Dr. Colter."

"Slow down, Blake. Tell me a little more before I jump out of bed and into my car to interrogate some drunk doctor from the bar."

"Trust me, Billy, he treated Janie in his clinic. I am pretty sure it was that same night. Here's the thing. I did not want to make him nervous and ask too many questions while he was here with his buddies. I got his driver's license and have our guy driving him home. I'll make sure he pops him something to wake him up a bit so we can talk to him. He is a talker and not happy about how Janie was treated. I think the guy was coerced into treating her, but let's find out."

"I hope you're right about this, Blake. It would certainly be nice to know Chase's hunch was right and find a clue to her whereabouts. I'm on my way now."

Colter stumbled into his dimly lit house and was surprised at how wide awake he felt. He was thankful for the ride home and sure all the guys had a great time. Just as he was about to close the door, he felt it jam. Looking down in his tipsy state, he saw a black shoe. Stepping away from the door, Colter saw the formerly friendly bartender and another man step through the door. Both had serious looks on their faces.

Trying not to scare the drunken doc right away, Blake smiled and said, "Glad you made it. That beautiful woman you treated happens to be a friend of ours." Pointing at his boss, he asked, "Can you let Billy here know what you told me about the night you helped her out?"

Knowing he could not run or backpedal himself out of the situation, Colter sat on his chair and put his hands on his face as if he were massaging his brain for answers. In truth, he wanted to talk about this bothersome situation or he wouldn't have blabbed it to the bartender in the first place. First, he needed to be assured that these guys had as much or more clout than his "friend" Marco.

"What is your interest in the girl?"

At that, Billy knew right away that he had information and wanted to back him into the wall and stick a knife to his throat but knew he wouldn't get that far with this wimpy guy. He'd probably pass out and they'd need to wait hours for him to wake up. So, he took another approach.

"She's a relative and in a heap of trouble. We need to find her if she is still alive."

They hit the jackpot with Colter, as he was totally unfiltered. "Jesus, I should've called someone about this, but I thought they'd kill me. They brought her to my clinic a couple of months ago; she was unconscious and had a gunshot wound. She looked so frail, and these guys were ruthless. If they could talk about ending the life of that beautiful, harmless girl so easily, I knew they'd have no qualms about slitting my throat. Marco is the only reason I'm still alive. Here's the thing: if I give you the information you need, can you keep those guys from me?"

Billy was ready to beat the shit out of him right then and there, but thought they may need him down the road. He played the powerful nice guy card, trying to sound as legitimate as possible.

"Of course, Dr. Colter. Sounds like these guys are bad news. How do you know them? Where are they from? You mentioned the name Marco." He inched closer, intimidating the good doc.

"Well, uh . . . I served in the Gulf War with Marco. He saved my life a long time ago and now decided to call in a big favor. Really, I thought I'd be killed if I said no and I also knew I could help the girl better than some chop shop they may have taken her to otherwise. Marco Diego is the only name I know. I don't even know where they took her or anyone else. The girl woke up very confused. I'm not sure what sedative they gave her, but I was worried she would not come out of it for a while. She seemed to have amnesia at first or perhaps was in shock. Two men were in with her for a bit and I am pretty sure she could hear them discussing her fate. I could tell Marco knew her and was fond of her. He was rooting for keeping her alive. As soon as she came to, she acted as if she had no idea what happened to her and kept asking about her car and an accident by her father's house. She called herself Janie at first, but they all called her Ella. As soon as I mentioned Janie, she gave me a look and said she had no idea why I'd call her that name. Getting the feeling that amnesia would help her case, I went with it. When I was alone with her, I mentioned that she better keep her story straight. They were very connected and dangerous."

"Keep your mouth shut, Colter. No more benders and you'll be fine. We hear of any stories—and we *do* have ears all over Vegas— you'll hear from us again and it won't be so nice. Are we clear? By the way, we do want to help her. You can feel that you did a good thing here tonight," said Blake.

Billy added to ensure his silence, "We're not just talking about your license, Doc. Keep your mouth shut." With that, they turned and walked out the door, leaving Colter stunned.

Chapter 44

WELCOME RETURN

T he timing of Chase's call to Blake was impeccable. He and Billy were about to call him the next day and give him the good news.

"Where are you, Chase? Still talkin' to the birds?" Blake chuckled.

Chase was such a city boy that neither really thought he'd make it in Costa Rica for more than a week. The fact that he lasted seventy-five days showed his intensity, focus, and patience. He adapted to his surroundings well, but was about to jump out of his skin.

"I'm heading to the fucking airstrip to get on a plane, hoping I make it over the damn mountains without crashing into one, getting stranded, and resorting to eat the lone, fat pilot until you assholes rescue me. I'm getting outta this jungle, so you'd better have some good news or hide me somewhere else where I can at least see some buildings."

"We think Janie is alive, Chase."

Without waiting for a response, Billy got on the phone and explained what happened with Blake and the doctor.

"Here's the thing, Chase. The guy Marco works for is connected to some very interesting friends of ours, including your 'Uncle' Mac. We hear our mystery guy is in Washington working on making some controversial policy changes. We aren't sure if his connections are to you or Janie, so you are not out of the woods just yet. This is complicated. Get to the airstrip. We'll fly you into San Diego and have a driver get you home. I'll keep you out of the Vegas airport for now, and you can stay at my cabin in Mount Charleston."

Trying to take in the information, Chase began believing in a future again. Finally, he sucked in a breath and stammered, "So, you're saying this guy treated her that night but has no idea where they took her or if she's still alive?"

"Better than what I thought happened that night, Chase. You know, you were right about the lone ambulance driver. I promise we're on it. By the time you get here, we'll have more on Marco anyway. He's well connected. We just need to find out if he's working on the same side as our friends or secretly against them."

Chase felt a genuine smile on his face for the first time since he last smiled at Janie. He'd think positively until he had other proof. By the time he boarded the small plane, he decided he'd enjoy the view and anonymity. Again, his mind wandered to the idea of this situation somehow being linked to Janie. He could not imagine anyone killing such an amazing woman. The more he thought about it, he was sure she was running from something or to some other place. He knew he'd find her with this new lead. Mac's guys could find anyone if they had a name. Janie Blue might as well have been Jane Doe, but the name Marco Diego could produce some results.

Chapter 45

DEEP WITHIN

When the world feels like it's crashing down, somehow people find the strength from deep inside to keep going. Ella would barely make it through the next tragedy in store for her. If it weren't for the baby to protect, she would feel utter despair.

Late summer was a perfect time for Mike Ross, Ella's father, to do work around the house. The weather was fantastic on the island. With the sun shining, he thought about calling Dan before starting his busy day of repairs. Ever since Ella had come home, Mike could not stop feeling guilty about never discussing her adoption and her biological mother's death. Although they felt they were protecting her from the psychological ramifications of such a tragedy, which she seemed to have erased, were he and Kate really protecting their own little bubble? Perhaps both of them had talked themselves into thinking this was best for Ella. In reality, confrontation and making waves was just not their thing. Kate would say, "Leave well enough alone" and "If it's not broken, don't fix it" more often than not. Today, Mike had made up his mind to talk to Dan about discussing

Ella's past with her. He did not want her to go in and out of an amnesiac state throughout her life. Maybe, this could be more serious and happen more and more often. Of one thing he was sure: Ella needed a specialist and a therapist to get through this. The doctor he met in Las Vegas seemed knowledgeable, but it was Vegas, for God's sake. They were not known for their amazing hospitals. He drank his coffee and called Dan.

"Hey, Mike, how are things across the Sound? You ready to enjoy the beautiful day?"

Mike answered, "Yes, in fact, I am going to be the handyman and clean out the gutters for the fall rains. There are only so many dry, sunny days here to get these chores done."

"Right. Do you need any help? I can send someone out that way later."

Although thankful for the offer, Mike chuckled at the fact that his son-in-law never got his hands dirty. "No thanks, Dan. I enjoy doing these things myself. Keeps me busy and physically fit. We old guys need all the help we can get," he joked. "Hey, I do have something a bit more serious to talk to you about." Hesitantly but with conviction, he said, "Dan, I am hoping to have you and Ella over to dinner tomorrow night and discuss her adoption, amnesia, and past with her. I've decided that I cannot keep this from her, especially if she has recurring issues or if this is a serious medical condition we have missed."

Totally caught off guard, Dan had to think fast. "Mike, you know I have her under the best care. Maybe you can wait on that thought for a bit. Let's make sure she can handle this so soon after Kate's death."

"No offense, Dan, but Kate was my wife," Mike responded defensively. "It seems as if Ella is doing okay at the moment. She is about to accept chairing Project Hope. She is fully involved with kids that she may be able to identify with even more after understanding her past. She is a strong and grown woman, you know. I am not sure you're giving her the credit she deserves."

Understanding what he needed to do, Dan carefully agreed to Mike's plan and said they'd be there for dinner tomorrow. All the while, he knew full well there would be no dinner with Mike ever again. His next call was to Marco. He needed another favor.

Chapter 46

HIDDEN DECEPTION

L ater that day, Mike had all the tools he needed on the roof at the rear-facing side of the house. He needed the ladder to stay over on the east side of the house since the back was nestled in the trees. That side dropped off down the hillside pretty steeply. So far, Mike had sprayed most of the gutters clean of debris and leaves. Just as he moved carefully toward the back of the house, his power washer went on unexpectedly and spooked him. It wrapped around his leg and knocked him off the roof. As he fell, Mike saw a man's figure by the side of his house. Tumbling off the roof and down the steep hill was not what killed Mike Ross. It was the final blow to his head that sent him to see his lovely wife.

The man checked his vitals, took the sharp, bloody rock, and put it in his car to hide any evidence. As he was leaving the gravel drive-way of the hidden-away property, he passed a woman in a vintage Mustang convertible. He sped away not knowing that she was calling on Mike Ross. It seemed she, too, was concerned about Ella and had planned on meeting with her best friend's father. Luckily, Stacey had not told Mike what she knew as of yet or she could have had an accident as well. Driving up to the house brought up so many fun childhood memories of playing hide-and-seek on the huge property, collecting rocks down the hill by the water, and sitting on the big tire swing, talking about boys and drinking lemonade or, later, spiked lemonade. She hadn't noticed the fallen ladder but did notice water spraying in the air. At first, she thought it was a broken sprinkler. As she got out of her car and moved closer to the side of the house, she knew something was wrong. The power washer had knocked out a window and was spraying uncontrollably.

She called out, "Mr. Ross? Mike, are you up there? Are you okay?"

Then she ran into the house to see if he was there or perhaps if someone was helping him with chores around the home. Suddenly, her heart raced and her doctor's instinct kicked into high gear. She looked around the back, steep side of the house and saw a broken gutter. She followed the hill down, as she could see something below. It was Ella's father lying still. Immediately, Stacey checked his pulse and found none. She performed CPR and got no response. Seeing the huge gash on the back of his head led her to believe that Mike Ross was not coming back. She sadly called 911. Her next call would be much more difficult.

192

Chapter 47

MORE BAD NEWS

T he last nine days had almost pushed Ella over the edge. Dan maintained his role as a sexually charged, narcissistic asshole every night. He was sure that he saw her fear and loved every minute of it. It turned him on when she tensed up if he touched her. Unfortunately, it was a mechanism she could not turn off within herself. She was certain that if she acted as though she wanted more, he would lose interest in her. There was also a look in his eye that indicated he was waiting for her to slip. At least his excitement for her would keep her alive long enough to find a way to save herself and her baby. If he thought this baby was his even for a while, he would not harm her. Her dad left a message on her phone that he wanted the two of them to come to dinner tomorrow evening. He said he had some important things to discuss. She would break the news of the baby to both of them after dinner.

Having her dad's knowledge of her pregnancy would help make everything seem normal. She decided to take a walk outside and get some fresh air. As usual, she took her cell phone along. Just as she was about to switch on the CD Walkman clipped to her waistband, a call came through from Stacey. Well, maybe she'd just have a girl chat on her walk. Instead, she answered the phone to Stacey's panic-stricken voice.

"Ella, where . . . where are you right now? Is anyone with you?"

"What is going on, Stace? I am a block from my house about to take a nice walk. Are you okay?"

"I'll be right there. I am ten minutes away." She hung up the phone.

This was unlike Stacey. Ella walked back to the house prepared to hear about a sudden breakup or something horrific that had happened at the office. Five minutes later, she saw her friend drive up in her red Mustang convertible. She looked pale and clearly came with bad news. Ella braced herself, but not physically. Stacey walked inside and could not hold back tears as she saw her friend. This was not a doctor talking to a patient's family at the hospital. She was about to tell her that as of today, she no longer had a sole living parent or relative. This man was amazing; he was like a father to Stacey. Sadly, her father had died when she was a baby. Mike Ross always made sure to give her advice and help. Stacey's mother had sworn her to secrecy but wanted her to know that Mike had helped pay for her medical school tuition. He was the nicest man she knew, with the biggest heart in the world. Shaking, but making sure they were both sitting down, Stacey held her friend's hands and gave her the life-altering news.

"He must've fallen from the roof, Ella. I am sure he was cleaning out the gutters and it looked like the power washer malfunctioned and maybe caught him off balance. He fell and hit his head. I'm so sorry, honey," she said, breaking between tears. "I performed CPR, but it was no use. He was gone."

Ella looked straight at Stacey and, putting both hands on the arms of the chair, stood up. Ella was about to give her friend a hug but fell to the floor like a ragdoll right in front of Stacey. It was so unexpected that Stacey's reactions were not fast enough to catch her.

Immediately, she knew Ella was in shock and got her to the guest bedroom and put blankets on her. She was so cold. Stacey was the only one who knew about the pregnancy—and its importance. She called Dan and told him what had happened to Mike and then to Ella upon hearing the news.

"Stacey, what were you doing at her dad's house anyway? Was anyone else around?"

Chapter 48

STATE OF SHOCK

hocked that Dan was not asking more about his wife's condition or her own state of mind after finding Mike's dead body, Stacey tried to maintain a calm attitude. She told him, "No one else was around, Dan, but I called 911 right away."

"Listen, do not call an ambulance for Ella. Sounds like she has fainted from shock, right?"

"That would be my diagnosis. Please hurry, so we can take her to Seattle General together, okay? I'll call ahead."

"Thank you, Stacey. I'm sorry you had to be the one to find Mike, but I'm glad it was you breaking the news to Ella," he said in the most charming voice he could muster.

Knowing the real Dan, she pretended to be charmed in order to help Ella. After ten minutes, Dan was at the door.

"Let's get her to the hospital quickly. Fill me in on Mike on the way." He put his head down and closed his eyes. "He was a great man. We'll get through this."

Stacey could see through his phony stammering, but pretended to have empathy for him. They got Ella into a room right away as Stacey's colleague did some tests.

"Ted, why don't you run a blood test. I want to make sure and rule out anything else. She hasn't sounded so great on the phone lately."

"Of course, Stacey. I'll be thorough." He called down to a nurse to draw blood. "I am certain she is in shock, so let's keep her warm and give her some rest."

Both her husband and her best friend waited in the room while they ran tests. The nurse came back ten minutes later and whispered something to Dr. Ted Bentley. He seemed to smile for a moment and asked for a minute alone with Dan. Stacey happily obliged, already knowing exactly the news he would give.

Dan sat down for a minute when the doctor asked him if he knew his wife was pregnant. "Uh . . . no . . . I hadn't even thought about it."

"Well, congratulations, Mr. Carmichael. It's probably in the very early stage, but the pregnancy was detectable through the blood test. I am sure part of her problem is exhaustion." He smiled.

Minutes later, Ella woke up. The doctor and nurse checked her vision and signs for a concussion. They asked her a few simple questions, then quietly left the room saying they would be back in a few minutes.

She looked at Dan as she blankly said, "My dad is gone, Dan. I feel like I can't breathe."

He came to her, hugged her, and let her cry. He would wait until she stopped before telling her about his baby she was carrying. To Dan, this meant his polls would go up. People loved to hear interesting stuff like this. Someone dies, and then they announce a baby. What could be better? He could see the headlines already.

"Ella, there is something else. They ran a blood test to rule things out and came up with some positive news. You are pregnant." Dan smiled sweetly just like a proud father-to-be.

Finally, her secret was out. She'd hoped the timing was okay and made sense. Dan did not seem to question anything. She tried to smile, but could think only of her father for the moment.

"Dan, I want to see my dad. Please, can we go?"

"Let's talk to the doctor, okay? You need to rest and eat something. Little Danny or Daniella needs some rest too. Sit tight. I'll be right back."

He left wondering if it was all of the power sex he was giving her that changed their luck. He knew that idiot bitch doctor years ago was wrong about his "slow swimming" sperm. He had never told Ella this and never would. He'd show them all.

Stacey walked in after Dan left. Ella told her what he'd said.

"There is so much to think of and be sad for that I just want to focus on this little person inside. I wanted to tell my dad tomorrow night at dinner. He wanted to discuss something important. Do you know anything about this, Stacey?"

Unsure what to do with the confusing information in her mind right now, Stacey shook her head back and forth. "No, sweetie, I do not. You really do need to get rest. They'll give you something safe for your condition that will help you sleep, all right? You've had a hell of a couple months, haven't you? Here comes Ted. He's a great doc. Right, Dr. Bentley? You'll take care of my girl and hers?"

With true sincerity, he said, "I am so sorry about your father, Ella. At the same time, I want to congratulate you on your pregnancy. Your husband looked happy. I am sure this is a strange moment for you, but you've got to focus on this baby and get your rest and lots of liquids."

He gave her something to help her sleep. It was the first pill she had taken since the "incident" almost eight weeks ago. This, she did because her friend was there to check on not only the pill but also Dan's reaction.

Stacey turned to her colleague and asked, "I'll get her to cooperate, Ted. Give us a minute."

He left and she turned to Ella, handing her the pills and telling her, "Seriously, El, you need major rest. We'll talk about the monumental injustices in life tomorrow." She bent down to say softly as her voice cracked, "I felt your dad lingering, Ella. He's here and would want the very best for you." At precisely that moment, the lights flickered at the unexpected preluding storm outside.

Both women looked at each other and nodded their heads. It was the only light moment they would feel for weeks to come.

"Tomorrow is another day, right? Isn't *Gone with the Wind* one of your favorites? I will see you then. Sleep tight," she whispered, leaving Ella to her peace and quiet.

The last person to see Ella that night was Dan. He stood over his lovely wife feeling more powerful and centered than he felt in a long time. Finally, she would need him and rely on him for everything. Twistedly, he thought that with her parents gone, he would be the center of her universe. Hopefully, that nosy bitch Stacey would stay out of the way. He would find out for certain whether she had seen anything suspicious at Mike's home when she found him. With Ella sleeping so peacefully, he decided to place a hand on her belly. In a strange, protective instinct, Ella's eyes flew open, startling Dan. Slowly, she closed them after staring straight into Dan's eyes like a mother wolf when confronted by danger, protecting her pup.

Chapter 49

A FALL TO BREAK

The heat was rising even as the sun went down in Vegas. It had been the hottest September they could remember. Temperatures were also rising among the group of men gathering information for O'Shea as something big was happening at Hotel Du Monde.

Billy was fervently working with the casino upper echelon to coordinate and avert chaos for the upcoming fall tourist season. He was constantly the go-to guy who mediated various top casino bosses so they all came out smiling. Smiling to them meant huge profits. Now that Billy and Chase were diligently conspiring to locate Janie, they realized how well they worked together. Chase already had great relationships with many of the owners and their right-hand people, but Billy added tenfold to his credibility. Now, he knew the inner workings almost as well as Billy. Almost. Billy was grooming Chase to take over some of his accounts, yet create his own niche. This meant security. These days, the entire success of any casino depended upon absolute security in areas of technology, disasters, finances, and catching major players always looking for a way to cheat the system.

The past week, Billy seemed very tired and went home early. Not his usual routine. Today, they had a big meeting to work out some of the final kinks in O'Shea's plan. During one of their typical morning coffee meetings, Billy ordered an extra couple of espresso shots as a pick-me-up. He needed to be fully focused at the meeting. Before they got started, Blake called Billy.

"Blake, is it important? Chase and I are preparing for an important gig."

"Yes. I know who this Diego character is. R. J. Davies ring a bell to you? Used to be friends with Mac and . . ."

"I know who the hell he is, but how are they connected?" Billy answered angrily, holding his left arm in slight pain.

Chase saw his face go pale as he clutched his left arm and squinted, still listening to Blake. He ran over to the barista, who yelled to a regular in the corner who happened to be a doctor. Chase also flagged him down just as the guy was looking at Billy intently. He rushed straight over just before Billy collapsed and stuck a pill in his mouth, making him chew and swallow it down. The manager had already made the call to 911. An ambulance came a few minutes later. They took him to Sunrise Medical, which was the nearest hospital and better equipped to deal with cardio and stroke issues.

Chase waited in the designated room until a doctor finally came out. "He's a lucky guy, for sure. The fact that there was a doctor in the café saved his life. We'll keep him here for a few days to see what is going on and slow him down a bit, all right? Mr. O'Shea called and wanted us to keep him as long as possible, but I don't think Mr. Martinelli will stand for that." He chuckled. As an afterthought, he said, "Oh, he wanted me to give you this. Said it's important."

"Can I talk to him now?"

"Sure, just keep it mellow."

"Jesus, Billy, I knew you wanted a break, but the hospital?" Chase always tried to make light of any tough situation.

"Cut the crap, Chase. Before anything else happens to me in this shithole, I need you to take that to my attorney, Robert Mackie. It gives a few buildings and things to Janie. If anything happens to me, I want you delivering this, got it? Otherwise, there's no chance in hell that girl will accept it or come back here."

"It's a deal, Billy. Only, there's a catch. You need to stay here three days and try to chill out. I'll leave right now. O'Shea wanted to send a few ladies over to pamper you, but we thought that may cause some problems with the docs. So, we'll let them do their job, and I will do mine, including handling this and talking to Blake. I'll fill you in tomorrow, okay? Take it easy."

"Yeah, yeah—get to work."

As soon as Chase was outside of the hospital, he dialed Blake's number.

"I thought you'd never call. How is he?"

"He'll be fine if he can try and slow down. Man, he was really lucky. Any new information?"

"I think I found Janie. Come by the bar and I'll give you the details." He hung up right after that without saying more.

Chase practically ran to his new Jeep, jumped in, and floored it to the Pioneer Bar. Wanting the fastest route, he took the highway today. He was amped up and ready to drive to see her, wherever that may be. The last couple of months had felt like years. While in Costa Rica, he had gotten confirmation that his funds were in his offshore account from the Du Monde deal. He had already ruled them out regarding the hit, but it was nice to be sure. They never would have paid him had they planned on killing him. The jury was still out on Global Insurance. They had not asked him about another job yet but had also paid him his fee. Had he warned them against binding the casino, his fee as a percentage would have been far greater. For these reasons and the mere fact that Du Monde was their bound client now, Chase began to rule them out as his enemies. At least for now. So, it pointed to someone affiliated with Janie. She was the key to a couple of things. She unlocked some crazy chemistry and emotions within Chase, but also was most likely indirectly with someone out to kill Chase and harm her. As soon as he found out her whereabouts, Chase would get some answers.

As the dust flew upon his arrival at the Pioneer Bar, Blake met him at the door. They shook hands and Blake gave him a hearty pat on the back.

"So, how's the man dealin' with the white coats?"

"Billy is already ordering everyone around and trying to figure out how to get out of there before sundown. I think O'Shea has slightly more pull with the hospital staff, though, and may win this one." Chase laughed thinking about Billy trying to leave with him before handing him a note for Janie.

Blake saw Chase's anxious face and got right to the point: "So, here's the latest on your gal. We found this guy Marco up in Seattle. Through some of our friends, we learned he works for some powerful people. He's definitely trying to get some specific bills passed by making sure that a certain politician gets elected. Well, looks like his guy is a top candidate and also—brace yourself—is married to Janie."

"What the hell?" Chase said, shocked. "Do you have pictures? I need to see them together."

"Yeah. I have more than that. Here's a clip of him accepting the nomination for senator just two days ago. She is standing next to him. I will say, she looks pretty sad or maybe sick. You check it out."

He played the video clip. The new senatorial candidate, Dan Carmichael, looked like a typical eager, good-looking politician. Waving to the crowd, he seemed completely pleased with himself and did not once glance at Janie. She smiled very demurely, not at all full of bright smiles he had seen or the slightest hint of happiness or mischief. Dan had to be the reason behind everything. Well, he and this guy Marco.

Looking pissed off and uneasy, Chase turned off the computer. "What do you think, Blake? She looks exhausted with dark circles and did not once look at her husband, who has just won a major political race. Tell me what else you've heard."

"Sounds like her father just had an accident and died. Her mother died two months ago, just before you met her. In fact, days before you two met. I am not sure about the coincidence of her parents' deaths, but I am pretty sure about one thing: Marco could have her killed in a second if he thought she knew too much. I get the feeling from a couple of sources that Carmichael's election would help some powerful people or make them a shitload of money. It seems most of these entitled pricks have a woman behind them, so for now, maybe she's necessary to their strategy."

"I'm going to see this for myself. Now. Do you think her story about amnesia rings true? She did not look like the same woman to me, although she's still gorgeous. So, her name is Ella, huh? That name doesn't fit her. Let's wait for Billy to get out of the hospital before throwing all of this at him. I'm heading up the coast for a drive."

"At least you didn't say you'd be on a plane. We need you to lay low. Keep yourself out of trouble, Chase. Just watch her and gather information. I don't want your face in front of them yet. It would be a whole lot better for them to still think you are dead. It's not this idiot politician that worries me but those who Marco works for. Got it?"

"You done playin' my mother, Blake? I know where you're coming from and will do my best to stay out of the limelight. I just need to see her and see if she remembers me. She could be in big trouble as we speak or in the future. Once he is elected, will they really need her? By the way, can you get this to Mackie ASAP for Billy? I have other things to take care of, but I promised I'd get this done. Today, right?"

"No problem, Chase. I've got a couple of other things for him anyway. I'll hook up with him today and say it's urgent." He nodded to Chase, gesturing a half-assed salute.

After leaving the bar, Chase gathered a few things together, gassed up his new Jeep, and prepared to drive through the night and day until he made it to Seattle. He knew Blake would keep him posted on any new, useful information. He could not keep his mind from wandering to the haunted look on Janie's—or Ella's—face. She looked beautiful and yet so tired and sad. Her hair was cut in a long bob and beautifully waved around her pale face. She had been dressed in a tailored, light-yellow suit, showing off her petite figure. The press discussed her role in Project Hope, which was about the only time she smiled genuinely. He wanted to freeze that frame in his mind. From the moment he met her, she was the most relaxed woman he had ever met, with a brilliant and easy smile that made you melt. Perhaps this was because she felt she had nothing to lose or was momentarily free from whatever demons haunted her. Thinking of her made him step on the gas.

The next morning, Billy called Blake. He was feeling better and ready to get the hell out of the hospital. "Why isn't Chase answering his phone?" he asked, irritated.

"It's a long story, Billy. Why don't I pick you up and we can get you up to speed. A lot happens when you are sleeping," he teased.

Exhausted from the drive, Chase checked into a tiny cash-only motel outside of Seattle, slept for a few hours, and took a shower. Afterward, he powered down a cup of coffee and jumped back in his Jeep, headed toward the city to find the woman he was now convinced he loves.

Chapter 50

SWEET JANE

At times, dreams create an illusion more vivid than reality. Depression pushes a person to escape to the colorful place where they sleep or run from the nightmare back to life as they know it. Unfortunately, reality may be their living nightmare. Ella was lying in the hospital, sleeping hard yet feeling as if she could touch everything in her dream. She saw images of her mother, Eliza, laughing, and her adopted mother, Kate, looking at Eliza. Her father joined them. Strangely, they all talked and laughed as if they were old friends. Their surroundings were that of a country setting near a river. The sun was shining, and they were dressed for church. Someone she did not recognize came out to join them. He looked like a priest about to perform a ceremony. He was smiling down at a tiny, fragile baby with dark hair in his arms.

He put a few drops of water onto her forehead and then all of her parents came forward. First, Eliza held the beautiful baby in her arms, rocking her gently. Next, she passed her to Kate and Mike to hold and ogle over. In her dream, she heard a loud noise like thunder and everyone disappeared. Ella woke up, startled by the thunder out-side and sad to leave the comfortable dream where her parents looked so happy. She felt so tired, queasy, and extremely thirsty, as if she'd been in the desert without water for a day. Pushing the button next to her, she called the nurse, hoping to get some water. With her hand on the button, she passed out. The nurse ran into the room to find Ella in a pool of blood.

Immediately, the nurse, knowing who her case was, could tell she'd had a miscarriage. But there was more blood loss than usual. Her patient lay unconscious. She got the doctor in the room straight away. After they gave her more intravenous fluids for her dehydra-tion and stopped the blood loss, they felt assured she would be okay physically. The nurse could not help thinking that this poor girl would have an emotional crisis on her hands. She had heard that her father had died the previous day, just prior to her being brought in. Belinda was a heavyset nurse with a huge heart and a contagious smile on her face. All her patients usually left the hospital feeling a little better because of her vibrant personality and loving care. She thought she'd really have to work some magic with this young lady.

Belinda picked up the phone to call the two numbers listed as emergency contacts. Her husband, Dan Carmichael, the charming politician she had seen in there earlier, of whom her patient looked frightened, was one. The other name, listed as "friend," was Stacey Rollings; there were four different numbers next to it. She thought she'd seen Dr. Rollings slide into the waiting room after visiting hours were over. Just a hunch, but she checked to see if she was still there even before calling her husband. There was nothing like a girl-to-girl talk, especially in these cases. Sure enough, Stacey was curled up on the small, uncomfortable vinyl couch, using her sweatshirt as a pillow.

Belinda gently woke her up and whispered, "Stacey? I thought since you were still here and you're her 'doctor,' I would let you know about your friend, Ella."

Stacey braced herself as the look in the nurse's eyes was very sad.

"She had a miscarriage. She could use her friend when she wakes up."

Stacey was beside herself with grief for her friend. She just did not know how much more Ella could handle. Belinda let her in the room to wait until Ella woke up. Next, she called her husband.

Stacey really hated that guy. Everything around Ella was crumbling because of him. She even had her suspicions about what happened to Mike, Ella's father, which she kept to herself. It did not make sense that someone was leaving the drive about the same time he fell to his death. She'd known how agile and handy Mike was; he'd worked on their home for years without much help. He needed landscapers, as the grounds were huge, but she and Ella would laugh at him, especially when he'd try to fix the sink. Among themselves, they fell down in fits of laughter at the thought of Mike Ross with a potbelly and a plumber's crack!

The sheer coincidence and timing of the other car suddenly leaving had made her suspicious. She wanted to go back without alerting the police to see if she could see exactly where Mike hit his head. There would be a rock or sharp object with blood on it. After she brought Ella to the hospital, Stacey called an ex-girlfriend of hers who used to be on the force and now worked for a private detective agency. They were still good friends. Stacey was still her "doctor on call" whenever she was too embarrassed to call her GP. Without giving her too much information, she asked her to follow Mike's "fall line" and see if she came up with anything that would've been the object that had gouged his head so badly. She had not heard back yet.

Just as she looked up from checking for any messages on her pager, she saw Ella awake and staring at her sadly.

"My baby's gone, isn't she, Stacey?"

"Ella, honey, I am so sorry." She walked over to hold her friend's hand and saw Dan standing in the doorway.

Behind Dan's phony sad smile, he was hiding resentment toward

Stacey. He could not stand the fact that she was the first one Ella called in any crisis. In fact, until recently, Ella rarely had devastation around her. Now, she was the constant center of attention. He wanted to share that spotlight with her.

He was muttering under his breath as he watched them through the window, "Every time I turn around, that dyke is trying to turn Ella her way."

He thought, next, Ella would be hitting the gay bars and causing all kinds of gossip. As he rubbed his finger and thumb against his chin, he was thinking of a way and good reason to off Stacey just like Ella's father and her "captor," among others.

Walking toward Ella, he looked genuinely sad, almost angry. "Can you give us a minute, Stacey?" he asked with more than a tinge of irritation.

"Of course." She turned toward Ella, saying, "I will come by and see you later after work, okay?"

Blankly, Ella stared ahead, mumbling, "Okay."

Ella just wanted to go back to sleep and stay that way for a very long time. Maybe forever. She was numb.

Putting on his best nice-guy approach, Dan tried to be empathetic. He wanted her back at home helping him celebrate his nomination for senator. Also, he wanted her. All of this drama and her frailty made her even more attractive to him.

As usual, Dan did not say the right thing. "El, we'll try again, okay? It was early on and these things happen. We need to focus on things like Project Hope. That will make you feel better and keep you busy." He kissed her on the forehead and went to hold her hand.

She glared at him with stifled hatred and pulled her hand back. Before saying anything, Ella turned her head from him and looked straight ahead in a dead stare. Dan did not deal well with other people's grief, sadness, or depression. It made him very uncomfortable. Also, he wouldn't admit it, but a small part of him knew he was responsible for this happening.

Instead of trying to comfort her further, he called the nurse in to get her something to drink and told her he'd be back later. Not once did he mention her father's death, nor did he discuss her feelings. Even in her state, Ella knew Dan was hiding something more. Closing her eyes, she wanted only to go back to the dream with her parents and baby to feel a sense of comfort. She was not one to give up, but at the time she was hopelessly depressed. Luckily for her, she had a strong sense of avenging those she loved. She would turn her full attention toward redefining divine justice aimed directly at her husband. She had nothing left to lose.

Chapter 51

DARK DAYS

Returning to her house filled Ella with emptiness. Dan put her things on the hall bench and watched her walk softly and dully upstairs saying nothing. Ella climbed into bed and fell asleep. With such heaviness upon her, she did not need the drugs they gave her to sleep. Still, she took them anyway. Why not, she thought.

Stacey called over and over. Finally, Dan answered in an irritated voice, "Dan Carmichael." As if he did not know who was calling.

What an ass, Stacey thought to herself. Knowing that he would never let her get close to Ella if she did not play to his ego, she decided to compliment him.

"Hey, I saw that piece on the local news about you. You had conviction and a very nice smile. I'm sure it's been difficult for you lately, Dan. How are you holding up?"

Dan was surprised at her interest in him and appreciated the compliment. Not wanting to admit it, he did think the bitch might be the only person to talk some sense into Ella. He needed Ella to handle her father's service gracefully and, of course, stand next to him at his acceptance speech.

Reluctantly, Dan asked Stacey, "Do you think you could come over, Stacey? She's in bad shape."

Trying not to sound too eager, she said, "Of course, Dan. I'll try to get her smilin' again. How about in an hour?"

"Fine, but I cannot promise she'll be awake. I hope she doesn't grow too fond of the Ambien or whatever sleeping pill they've given her. See you then, Stacey."

Stacey threw on some clothes. It was her day off, so normally she sat in her pajamas until noon. She wanted to stop by the bakery and grab Ella's favorite cinnamon rolls and pick her up a latte just before going over there. Depression was a tough one to kick. Ella had suffered so much loss. Her ties to her parents and sense of duty remained very strong. Stacey felt she could use Ella's Catholic guilt to push her to focus on her father's funeral and kick her butt into gear. As she knocked on the door, it struck her how incredibly quiet it was around the house. She could hear the leaves rustling down the street in the wind. The mist had started, and the damp air chilled her to the bone. Waiting outside the door, Stacey brushed her blond curls from her face and pulled the trench coat around her sweats. She was thankful for her few extra pounds today. The combination of wind and humidity really seemed to cut right through her.

Just as she raised her fist to knock a bit louder, Dan answered the door. "She's upstairs" was all he could muster.

Stacey barely said hello and practically ran up the stairs. Surely, clunking up the hardwood staircase would awaken Ella. As she entered the room, Ella was in a deep sleep. It was obvious to Stacey that she had been abusing the prescription. It was no wonder, with what she'd been through. However, she had never seen Ella this low and needed to find a way to snap her out of this funk.

At first, Stacey brushed the waves out of her friend's face gently and said, "Ella, sweetie, you need to get up and talk to me."

When that did not work, she turned her over and lifted her eyelids.

She was out cold but just sleeping. She searched the room and bathroom for sleeping pills among other things, grabbed whatever she could find and headed downstairs to speak with Dan.

"Listen, Dan, I am going to throw these away. When she wakes up, page me, okay? I'll run some errands nearby."

Dan listened, as she was his only hope of getting Ella to look even halfway presentable to the public. For the time, he'd put off worrying about Stacey as a threat regarding his hand in Ella's father's death.

"Fine, I will find you when she awakens." Begrudgingly, he added, "Thank you."

Chapter 52

PICKING UP THE PIECES

Ella did not want to wake up. She felt like Sisyphus being punished for something she had done in life. Like the myth, that damn rock kept falling back on her, but now she wasn't sure if she had the energy or desire to change course or if she would just sit down with the rock at her back and take a *long* nap until the hill eroded. By the time she woke up, her mind was made up. She would find another way to fight back. Her head pounded as she struggled to get out of bed and wake up before her body was ready. Dan heard her movement and called Stacey right away. Fortunately, Stacey was around the corner making calls and came within minutes.

As Ella entered the kitchen, she thought they were about to have an intervention. Instead, Stacey and Dan pretended it was a casual meeting and that Stacey just came over to check on Ella. She would go along with it, because she needed to speak with Stacey alone.

"Good morning, Stacey . . . Dan. I need a stronger coffee. Do you feel like one, Stacey?"

That was their cue to get out of the house.

"I always do, Ella. Let's go. My car's out front." With that, they left Dan feeling uneasy yet slightly relieved.

Stacey looked at her petite friend with the dark circles under her eyes and the disheveled hair. She said, "El, it's time for a talk. We need to get it together for your father. His funeral is in three days. On top of that, you have a few engagements with Dan that you'll have to decide whether or not to partake in. One of them is his nomination ceremony."

Stacey thought she had better wait until Ella had her coffee before discussing her suspicions about any funny business surrounding Mike's death.

"I know, Stacey. I also know that I need out of this situation or I will die one way or another. Either he will get rid of me or I won't be able to handle living with such grief. Revenge is the only thing keeping me going at the moment."

Stacey was not at all about pussyfooting around and never acted or believed Ella was fragile. However, today seemed difficult. She had never been through such loss and certainly not so much of it in such a short time. Her mother, father, lover, and unborn child— Stacey could not even begin to imagine. If revenge was the key to helping Ella push through her unfathomable grief, then she should learn of Stacey's recent discovery. Her detective "friend" had been poking around Mike's home and the scene of the accident.

Looking Ella in the eye, Stacey laid out her thoughts: "Ella, the day I found your father, a man came out of the drive as I was approaching. I did not quite put it together until I'd seen how serious the fall had been. Obviously, he had not hired anyone to help him. So, this coincidence bothered me. There was a large gash to the back of his head, which also struck me as odd. I could not see where he had hit anything, and the only blood was at the spot where he landed. My friend, Cheryl, you remember her? The investigator? Well, I am sorry, but I felt it necessary to have her look at the scene before crying wolf. Honey, she could not find where your father would have hit his head to deliver the kind of blow that caused his death."

Ella's head was spinning, and she had already caught up to Stacey's suspicions. "So, you're thinking someone hit Dad on the head to make sure he was dead? Was he set up? Why? There is no logic behind the reasoning."

She was deep in thought, and her face contorted as she realized something. "Stacey, my dad was at the hospital in Vegas. Do you think they were covering their tracks and eliminating evidence? Maybe he saw something else or had something to tell me. He trusted Dan. Oh my God! You cannot be involved one more second! I am going to say that I am sick of everyone babying me and need a break. You need to say that you have tons of work right now, and cannot handle my stress until I snap out of it. You must come up with something and act angry with me. Then, I want you to go on vacation somewhere, anywhere but here. Please, Stace?"

"Ella, I will not abandon you, but I will play along with the fight scenario. I need you to act like you're snapping out of this, okay? I cannot begin to fathom how horrible all of this must be for you, but I know that the only way to achieve justice is to be strong. Can you handle the funeral and Dan's inauguration and stay off the damn sleeping pills?"

Ella knew it was exactly what she needed to do to clear her head. She nodded yes, but reluctantly. They drove back to the house. In an effort to create drama and get Dan's attention, Ella slammed the car door and marched up the limestone steps and into her house, pretending to be hurt and angry with Stacey.

She could barely look at Dan, so she directed all of her anger toward her act. "I do not want to see her again, Dan. Please do not take her calls. I will be fine for my father's funeral and your parties, but I will not have anyone accusing me of abusing drugs or not handling my responsibilities. I have had too much sadness in the past two months, but I'll be fine. Are we on the same page?"

He was surprised at her edge and authoritative stance, yet happy that she was seemingly rejuvenated. He had already forgotten about the funeral but knew she needed to stand strong next to him at the nomination announcement. The press would be everywhere. He had seen the amazing poise Ella possessed over the years and thanked God he did not have her killed. She would attract empathy, and people would see her strength. This would reflect on them as a couple. The voters would feel sorry for what they had been through and praise the Carmichaels for their resilience. To Dan, this could help make his career, as long as she stayed on his side. From all angles, Ella seemed to have no recall of what had happened in Vegas. She seemed to be on his side, just very sad. Now, his only worry was her friend. He was having his "friend" watch both Mike Ross's home and Stacey. He felt confident about getting away with Mike's death until his acquaintance told him he had seen a red Mustang convertible on the road. Still, he was pretty sure Stacey was busy with work and helping Ella overcome her problems, not to mention her own lesbian love life, that she would never harbor suspicions about Mike's death. But he was covering his tracks just to be 100-percent sure.

The following week, Mike's funeral was well organized and beautiful. Ella was holding it together for her father.

She thought, "I will make sure Dan pays for this." At the same time, the music played "Let It Be," creating a moment of silent antithesis. She cared nothing for the irony of the situation. Her only focus was revenge.

Later that evening, Ella heard Dan humming "We Are the Champions." This seriously made Ella want to punch him in the face. He was an idiot who got voted into office to actually help change serious national policies. He was not only relatively ignorant but narcissistic and evil. *Just the kind of person we want in politics*, she thought sarcastically.

Instead of voicing that on the morning of his nomination, she put on a fake smile and asked Dan, "You ready for this, future Senator Carmichael?"

Smiling back like a kid in a candy store, Dan said, "You bet. How about you, Ella? Gonna put on your famous smile and show your pride today?"

She bit her cheeks and muttered, "We'd better leave now. Wouldn't want to be late," grabbing her pale-yellow knit jacket. She let her newly bobbed hair down and smoothed her silky waves. She looked to be the pillar of all things good and would tremendously boost Dan's likeability merely by standing next to him as his devoted wife.

The ceremony went off without a hitch. Ella found it hard to smile, but made certain she did so a couple of times. She hoped people felt this was due to her recent circumstances. All the while, she had no idea Chase was longingly studying her every gesture and planning inadvertently to alter her plans for revenge.

Chapter 53

FALLING UP

Each day became tougher than the next. Getting out of bed was difficult. Ella felt imprisoned by the heavy duvet. She knew she needed to snap out of this and stay alert. She was immensely worried about Stacey, who had not yet left town. Today, curiosity got the better of her. She had checked so many places for paperwork that would nail Dan forever, but she had not yet ventured into his closet. It was filled with well-organized suits and shirts arranged by color. Nothing was really out of place. Although . . . She knew Dan worked out daily, yet she saw his gym bag sitting in the corner untouched. In fact, come to think of it, she had noticed it there every day. She decided to snoop.

As she opened the bag, she saw only his Adidas running shoes and a red T-shirt. There was another pouch which she did not think to open at first until she noticed a piece of blue jersey stuck in the zipper. It was the same beautiful blue color as the dress she'd had on when she was with Chase. Panicked, she worked the stuck zipper back and forth, pulling on the material at the same time. Finally, it freed up and opened. Ella gasped as she saw the dress she'd worn the same night of the attack when Chase was killed at Dan's request. She took the dress out and shook it. Seeing the hole made from the gunshot that grazed her leg brought back painful memories. As she fluffed the dress, something flew across the room, landing in the corner behind her nightstand. Drawing closer, she saw the silver objects and immediately burst into tears. She could hardly breathe looking at the small jackpot and ace charms given to her by Chase earlier that unforeseeable night. She remembered exactly what he had said. They were perfect and held so much meaning. She cherished the gift more than any diamond in the world. Ella picked up the delicate charms and rubbed them lovingly and gently between her fingers. Then, she placed them in her pocket. She felt comforted just having them near.

Hearing an unexpected noise downstairs, she quickly put the dress back in the pouch and placed the gym bag exactly where she had found it. Throwing on some comfy sweatpants, she washed her face casually in the bathroom. As she pulled her hair up, she saw Dan in the mirror, studying her.

She did not want to be near the bedroom, so she quickly blurted, "Hey, I am rushing to a massage appointment. Remember, you thought I should relax and enjoy myself today?"

He seemed disappointed but somewhat pleased she was getting out of bed and looked slightly refreshed. He did not want a depressed case hanging around. Also, he needed her to begin working on Project Hope. Now that he was a shoo-in to be elected senator, he had higher aspirations.

"Have a good day. Have you thought about getting to work on the project again? I know they need to make a decision soon about who will chair it, but they have been giving you extra time. I don't think they can wait much longer, babe."

Once Ella left, Dan looked around the room and noticed nothing out of place. He decided to put in a call to Rory, his acquaintance responsible for Ella's father's death. Since Marco would have nothing to do with the murder and thought they could figure something out with Mike, Dan had taken measures into his own hands. He noticed Marco's quiet stares lately and really resented his defiance. He now had the power to make some important decisions for Marco and his friends. They had better respect him, he thought.

After only one ring, Rory answered in a whisper, "Finding out lots of information, boss. Looks like the cute doctor knows too much and has someone I know snooping around Ross's place. We need to talk about this," he insisted, hanging up curtly.

Rory was still somewhat of an amateur, moonlighting on the side while working for a shady investigator. This was how he knew of Stacey's friend, yet only because she worked with one of the best and most expensive outfits around.

Dan felt as if he'd been punched in the gut. As much as he would like Stacey out of the picture, he did not know how many more coincidences could happen before he got busted. He was just really moving forward in his political career. Unfortunately for Stacey, her findings, if checked out by authorities, could put him out of business and in jail for the rest of his life.

Chapter 54

SO CLOSE

C hase waited outside of Ella's home for a day and a half before seeing her sullenly walk down the front steps. Her hair was swept back in a ponytail with some wispy, wavy pieces falling out, framing her beautiful yet sad face. She looked quite a bit thinner, making him want to pick her up, pull her in his arms, and tell her it would all be okay. Although Chase knew she had suddenly lost both her mother and her father, he knew nothing about the miscarriage.

The guys back in Vegas and Chicago, meanwhile, were working on establishing a relationship with Marco. If they could get him on their side, it would be much easier to get Ella away from her scumbag husband. So far, Billy, Blake, and Marco were all connected, but needed to make sure they had a common goal. This took time and maneuvering, as they were also competitors in many illegal activities.

Chase followed Janie—Ella, he reminded himself—to a coffeehouse and waited for her to emerge. He wanted to catch her completely off guard in order to confirm whether she really had amnesia or discover what game she may be playing. As she slowly opened the door with a coffee in her hand, he almost jumped in front of her. She was shocked as if she'd seen a ghost, but she held herself together.

Breathing heavily from the shock of seeing the man she had fallen in love with—a man who was thought to be dead—standing in front of her almost knocked her off her feet. Without thinking, he picked her up, saying, "Janie Blue, I thought you were gone!" The rest was making her dizzy. Ella focused on the fact that some-one could be watching, which could inevitably kill them both. Her instincts told her to act as if she did not know him and stick with her story. So, she did.

"I am so sorry, sir, but you've mistaken me for someone else." She tried to sound indignant but failed. Just then, Matt, a police offi-cer and Dan's friend, walked up to intervene.

Chase simply said, "Sorry, miss" and disappeared while Ella chatted uncomfortably with Matt. She did not say one thing about the encounter except that a man bumped into her, spilling her latte. Her head was reeling as she desperately needed to know if that was a dream or a real occurrence. Was she becoming delusional in her desires after finding those charms earlier?

Meanwhile, Chase retreated discreetly and found somewhere to watch her every movement. Clearly, she was shocked. He could not tell if she was happy to see him alive or wanted nothing to do with him. She was definitely hiding her emotions carefully. It took every ounce of control for him not to put his arms around her tightly and kiss her right there for everyone to see. Knowing that his potential hit man could be around the corner even now, watching her closely, forced him to back down. Blake and Billy's sources told him that she would be in danger if anyone thought she remembered her past. They had kept a close eye on Dr. Colter.

Luckily, for Ella, no one was watching her lately. She seemed to be playing her part well. Shaken, but with a ray of hope that Chase was alive unless she'd imagined it, Ella took the steps up to her house two at a time. She needed to find out information and fast. In her excitement, she let down her guard. Pushing open the door to Dan's office, she made a beeline for his desk. She did not even notice how dark it was as the privacy shades were down. Rifling through drawers while trying to pick a lock, she heard a voice in the corner of the dark office. It was Marco.

"What the hell are you doing, Ella?" he muttered.

Knowing all the while she could not come up with an excuse fast enough, she had to try. "I . . . I need to find this information on Project Hope before they give away the chair position, Marco, and can't find it anywhere."

"Try again, Ella. You've never kept anything in his office. You and I both know this is sacred ground for Dan. Listen, before you rack your brain, let me tell you something." In all seriousness, he took a step toward her.

Ella braced herself as she was certain he was about to strangle her with his bare hands. She saw the letter opener but didn't think she could reach it from her position.

He switched on a small, dim light, leaned forward, and looked her straight in the eyes. "Ella, I am on your side, okay? I never tried to hurt you, but I have been on a sort of mission for some friends of mine who are very powerful. As it turns out, we messed with the wrong people in Vegas and we are trying to make amends. In saying that, various policies need to change, and your husband, however cruel, now has the power to help make that happen. Are you following?" He talked slowly to her as if he were speaking to a small child.

Looking around, still confused, Ella muttered, "Did you kill my father?"

"Absolutely not! I am looking into finding the coward that ordered that hit as we speak."

Feeling a little gutsier, she then pressed, "Are Chase and Billy dead?"

"No, but Dan believes Chase was killed. I knew amnesia was far-fetched but went along with it. Not only do I like you, but more importantly, I was sure we needed you in order to win the election.

Dan's an egotistical ass. Without a strong, empathetic woman on his arm, he would be very unbalanced. We are at a touchy time with a lot on the line right now. I need you to keep it together and Chase needs to go home. I think you know he's alive. He cannot be a hero today or he will be dead tomorrow. You need to find a way to strongly persuade him that you are not interested in him. I think he is outside watching you. I know that Dan is in a meeting for the next two hours. Do what you need to do, Ella."

She knew exactly what to say to get him to leave. Once alone with him, this would be one of the most difficult speeches to utter. All she really wanted to do was curl up into a ball and cry in his arms. She wanted to tell him how much she felt for him and what his loss had meant to her. Also, she wanted to talk to him about the baby they would never see together, and how it had given her the strength to move on when she needed it most, knowing that she was carrying and protecting his child. None of this would be said. Instead, what she must say to Chase would be cruel and unforgivable.

Marco told Ella which car he was in and where it was parked. She threw on a parka and practically ran out of the house. As conflicted as she was about her future actions, she did want to see him alive in person knowing that he was real. She opened the passenger door and sat down.

Immediately, he grabbed her hand and pulled her close to him kissing her hard on the lips. Unable to resist, she kissed him back for the tiniest of moments, but then pushed hard away and slapped him with all the anger and rage she felt for Dan that she could muster. Otherwise, she could never hit Chase and make it seem real.

"You bastard!" She said with her teeth clenched. "Stay out of my fucking life forever. You are linked with someone who viciously killed my mother. You must be so like him. I never, ever want to lay eyes on you again. I used you, you know, to track my mother's murderer. You are nothing to me." Saying this while crying unintentionally and almost out of control, Ella opened and then slammed the car door shut, running back into her house barely able to breathe. Knowing that would probably send him over the edge and back to Vegas for good was more than she could take.

Ella passed Marco and ran upstairs to her bedroom. She knew Marco was right and hoped he really was on her side. What he said made sense, and she could not fathom anyone else in her life getting killed in her wake. She hoped he would help find her a way out of this situation by controlling Dan.

Chase had a tough time with her words. There was a ring of truth in her sentiments and accusations, but more than anything, he wondered about her using him. He did not know how she sort of popped out of nowhere without giving him any information. Or, coincidentally, how Billy happened to be her mother's lover and killer. He had been trying to rack his brain over all the coincidences while he was in Costa Rica. He would leave for now, but he'd stay involved. His sources said that she was still in danger. He needed to get to the bottom of this for his own closure. She had a pull on him, and he was certain he'd seen her for who she was in Vegas. He did not quite believe her to be the actress type. When he kissed her, he felt absolute, perfect chemistry. Also, he wondered, why was it so hard for her to tell him off like that? During her outburst, she had no idea that he slipped the letter and titles to the bar and other properties from Billy in her coat pocket. Billy was not doing so well these days after his heart attack. Hopefully, she would find the letter and also a way to forgive him before he died. With that, Chase left. Not without one more look. He glanced up toward the window and noticed Ella watching him.

Chapter 55

CAT AND MOUSE

Heartbroken by the idea she had pushed Chase from her life forever, Ella watched from her bedroom window as he left. Although she wanted to get under the covers and cry or, better yet, take a sleeping pill and not think, she knew it was critical to check in with Stacey. At the same time, she needed absolute affirmation from Marco that Stacey would be left alone or protected. Ella could not handle one more person being hurt from her crazy actions over two months ago. Who would ever have thought so many lives would be altered by her dreamlike search for her past?

As she was dialing Stacey, she heard heavy footsteps coming up the stairs. Certain they were Marco's, Ella carefully put the phone down and walked toward her bedroom door. She opened the door, and he was standing there, looking somewhat angry.

"What is it, Marco?" she asked in a slightly shaken voice.

"Look, Ella, I know that was hard for you. I saw you in Vegas and thought you never looked happier or more relaxed since I have known you. Luckily, I never divulged this to Dan. Right now, I need to understand more about why you feel your father was killed. Your friend Stacey has some very interesting friends. If you want to work on the same side and keep you and anyone close to you safe, then I need to know everything you know. I don't know what kind of crap Dan is trying to pull. I think I know who he is working with to help him do his dirty deeds. The guy is an amateur, but ruthless. He has a couple of bad habits, so he really needs money. Let's find your friend before Dan gets back."

Ella felt she had no choice but to trust Marco. Hell, she was alive still and fully understood her role in getting Dan elected. She wondered who Marco knew and how they were connected to Billy and Chase. She wanted reassurance that they would be safe, too. She reached in the pocket of her parka for her phone and noticed an envelope. How she did not notice this before was beyond her. As she pulled it out, not caring that Marco was staring at her and waiting for a response, she saw Chase's unforgettable handwriting. The way he signed her name, Janie Blue, gave her chills. She knew she would need to read this later in private, and carefully pushed it back into her pocket so it wouldn't fall out. Grabbing her phone, she called Stacey. The call went straight into voicemail, so Ella left a quick, urgent message for Stacey to call her. She called her office as well and sent a message to her pager. She shrugged her shoulders at Marco, looking to him for advice.

"I think she is in danger, Ella. Dan has acted pretty paranoid and crazy. If this guy I think is involved, name's Rory, then he would want to act fast so as to get paid right away. He would convince Dan that she was snooping around and needed to be offed. He would not do anything in the city, her flat, or her office. It's too busy. She would need to be coaxed somewhere that an accident could occur. Think for a minute. What does your friend like to do or where does she go regularly that could be remote?"

"Oh my God, Marco! She has a boat. She's been known to take it out alone and at odd times. All of her friends and past girlfriends warn her not to. I know I've told Dan many times that I worry about this. Let's go! Now!!!"

The Puget Sound was not a place for boating amateurs. Stacey was a born sailor; both her parents loved the sport and the ocean. Her father was a commercial fisherman and her mother had a passion for sailing. The wind was fine this morning, but forecasters were calling for a storm later. Stacey was careful to track the weather but really needed some stress relief at the moment. Sailing made her forget about everything and relax. Although Ella told her to get out of town and take a trip, she knew there was no way she could leave her best friend during this crisis. Instead, she would hang at her little cabin on the island and sail. That way, she'd be close by if really needed. What she did not know was that she had been followed. She went into her cabin for supplies and to make a sandwich after completely checking and rigging her boat, Nellie Gray, named after her grandmother. At that time, Rory carefully and stealthily stretched the lines where she could not see until it was too late. He also messed with the rudder and small motor used for emergencies. The wind was picking up; ahead loomed a bad storm. No one was sailing. Rory could not have come up with a better accident had he tried. His job today would be easy. She would drown out there. If for some reason she did not, it would not come back as anything other than poor judgment on her part. He had just followed her here to see what she was up to and was presented with an opportunity.

Rory left the house unseen and grabbed his binoculars from the trunk. He drove to a lookout point where he could watch her flail in the water. She should never have hooked up with that snooty investigator who thought she was better than Rory. He'd need to find a way to take care of her too. This Dan was a gold mine. The jobs just kept coming in. Dan would probably tell Rory that he owed him one since he failed to cover his tracks. In any case, Rory had enough to blackmail Dan down the road to keep him happy for the rest of his life.

He watched Stacey set off sailing and thought, Wow, she is pretty good at this!

The wind took her far offshore. He looked up to the ominous clouds above, knowing the rain would start any minute. Seeing the line break and the boom knock her off the boat was enough for him. Earlier, he hadn't seen any other boats around. He felt sprinkles and heard thunder and was out of there with a smirk on his face.

Chapter 56

NO TIME TO BREATHE

"**D**ammit, Marco, start the engine. She's out there in this weather! Come on!" Ella barked, fearful for her friend's life.

"Calm down. I got it. Jump in!"

For a split second, she thought, *My God, maybe this is his brilliant plan to get rid of both of us.* The media would chalk it up to a crazy story about a friend trying to rescue her "B.F.F." and both getting in over their heads in the storm. Ella really could see the headlines now but decided not to worry. Her will to save Stacey was too strong. She quickly climbed in as they sped up to Puget Sound.

"Shit!" cried Stacey as the boom knocked her over. She got the wind knocked out of her for twenty seconds. Coughing up salt water in the midst of the angry waves while trying to find her way back to the capsized boat was the next task she struggled to accomplish. It was a losing battle, she thought. Thankfully, she religiously wore a Navy-certified life jacket. She was a risk taker but not stupid. Panicked, Stacey saw waves swelling on all sides of her and could no longer see the sailboat. She did not want to die out here, so she tried to conserve her energy by kicking lightly. She hoped the automatic alarm would alert the harbor patrol. The rain pelted down hard as the water rose, and she heard thunder in the distance. This storm turned nasty faster than she thought it would, and she wondered how long she had been in the water. Thinking she heard more thunder as her body temperature began dipping dangerously low, Stacey looked up to see a boat and felt large hands pulling her up. As she opened her eyes, Ella knelt next to her, wrapping blankets around her and telling someone else to take off the wet clothes. How the hell would she have known about her spontaneous sail? Stacey felt lightheaded but smiled at her friend who had always been there for her.

When they had seen the boat flipped over and almost underwater, Ella thought for sure Stacey was gone. They just kept circling the area and called for help. The harbor patrol was far off helping another boat that had gone astray. Finally, Ella saw the bright pink–and–yellow life jacket that her friend had always sworn was her lucky charm. Well, today she hoped she was right. When they reached Stacey, she was not moving and looked as if her eyes were closed. As Marco lifted her out of the water, she kicked her legs.

"What the hell are you doing out here, Ella?" She murmured in disbelief, almost inaudibly. "How did you know I'd be sailing?"

"Stace, let's just get you back to your warm bed and make sure you don't get hypothermia. We'll have a nice cup of hot tea and a talk. I am so happy you are okay."

They all went back to her cabin. Marco was a little reluctant but figured Rory must have left the scene after knowing she had been knocked off the boat. He had a pretty good idea where he'd go next, but he did not want to leave without the two of them. Surely, Rory would be covering his tracks and planning on eliminating the private investigator who had been Stacey's friend. In truth, Marco did not know what to do with that one. She knew too much. So did these two, but he thought they could be trusted. At least Ella promised him this was the case. He would keep an eye on Stacey but did not think Ella could live with another person close to her disappearing. That would not be good all around.

Soaking wet with chattering teeth in her heavy, wet parka, Ella grabbed one of Stacey's arms as Marco grabbed the other. Putting her arms around their shoulders, they walked Stacey from the boat to her cabin. Luckily, the heat was on as she must have been planning on staying the weekend. In fact, the refrigerator was stocked. Ella immediately put water in the kettle and started the stove. She did not want to explain the situation and circumstances of her accident until Stacey seemed stable with a warm cup of tea in her hand.

Chapter 57

BORN TO KILL

As Rory drove back toward Seattle, he felt good. Forget detective work, he could be a private assassin. Killing came naturally to him. He had parked up the hill from the home of Stacey's meddling friend, Cheryl. Her small Victorian house was in West Seattle, an artsy community near the beach recently dubbed as trendy. A lot of young families had begun moving to the area, but fortunately, Rory did not see kids around at the moment. School was in session. He was a sadistic bastard but still had a soft spot for kids. He was glad that she did not live in a busy area so he could watch the explosion from afar. Cheryl, the righteous bitch, he thought, strutted out of her house looking like she had some real good information for someone. Her boss, a sadistic woman in power, wouldn't even look at him for an interview a few years ago but might be in need of help after today. She opened the door to her BMW. He watched her adjust the rearview mirror, applying lipstick for the last time. As she turned the key, both she and her car ignited. Knowing there was no way anyone could live through that, Rory slowly turned down a side street and drove home to his apartment near Pioneer Square.

Marco got a message as the two women were talking, crying, and hugging. It said that his mouse was on the move again. He knew that meant Rory had killed the private investigator and was probably either heading home to his house, stopping by a dive bar, or stupidly trying to bribe Dan. He needed to stop him from the latter. Figuring out how to end his life would not be difficult if he headed toward his favorite hole in the wall off King Street. He had some ideas that entailed making some calls out of range of Ella and Stacey.

"Listen, you two, I am glad both of you are okay. Stay here until I call you. I need to tie some loose ends, all right?" He warned them with a pointed finger and serious look. He had actually begun to respect their strong sisterhood bond.

Both of them nodded. Ella started a fire as the rain came pouring down in buckets. With all of the excitement, she had forgotten about the formal dinner she and Dan were supposed to attend tonight. The only thing she wanted to do now was curl up on Stacey's couch and watch *Pride and Prejudice* with her friend. It was one of their favorite escapes.

After receiving the call that Rory had stopped for a drink at one of his regular haunts, Marco knew exactly what to do. He set him up. There would be someone to lure him toward a dark, deserted alley to buy some of his favorite drugs at low cost. It would look like another low-life drug deal gone bad. In the midst of his planning, however, Dan called him in a panic.

"Marco, where the hell have you been? I've been trying to reach you for the past two hours. Ella and I have a huge dinner for the Project Hope fund-raiser this evening. I can't find her. Have you been watching her?" he asked suspiciously.

"Yes, Dan, I have. She's fine. Just a little boat accident with her friend Stacey. I'll fill you in later. I think you should call and say she's feeling ill. She is fine, though. Can we talk in a couple of hours?" Marco tried to keep it light.

"What do you mean?? Why would she be on a boat?" Dan

stopped in his tracks as he realized this whole story did not ring true.

Marco did not know that Ella supposedly hated Stacey at the moment nor that she did not like or know a thing about boating. Ella was frightened of sailing. But Stacey did have a cabin where she sailed. Dan had a funny feeling that he was being set up. He would cancel the dinner and head toward the cabin unannounced to check on Ella and Stacey secretly.

Casually, Dan got off of the phone, saying to Marco, "You are right. I'll cancel for Ella and head to the dinner alone."

Hearing there was a message waiting, Dan checked a drunken voicemail from Rory. The message said in a slurred voice, "Blonds make terrible sailors." He understood right away yet was confused by Marco's message that Stacey and Ella were together and were fine after a small accident on the boat. Maybe Marco was covering for them. Dan had gone around Marco to kill Ella's father and knew his supposed right-hand man didn't agree with that decision. Something here definitely was not flying straight. Dan grabbed his car keys from the hook and took off in the rain at full speed, ready for a fight.

Hearing that his mouse was caught in an inescapable trap and feeling satisfied with Dan's dinner plans, Marco went for a quick whiskey. He needed to warm up and take a break from the crazy day.

About a half hour later, Marco rang Ella's phone, saying, "You forgot about the dinner tonight. I covered for you. Dan is going alone."

Shocked that Dan did not pitch a fit, Ella asked Marco just what he said to get her off the hook. As Marco let her know he talked of a boating accident with Stacey, Ella grew pale.

"Oh, no, Marco. He knows I hate boating! Also, at the moment, I am supposed to be in a huge fight with Stacey. It was the only way I thought to protect her before you and I spoke. I don't think he bought your excuse. Stacey and I need to leave."

With so much confusion, a crucial mistake had been made, and Marco felt sick. Now he needed to find Dan very quickly to make sure Ella would be protected. Dan would be furious if he thought

Ella and he were hiding something from him. He had to be stopped.

"Ella, I am on my way. Lock the doors, turn off the lights, and sit quietly in the bedroom on the floor until I get there. Do not answer your phone or the door." He figured he was about thirty minutes behind Dan if he was heading to the cabin. "Don't do anything crazy if Dan shows up. Just pacify him as long as you can. If you do anything rash, Ella, and policies don't have a chance of being changed for my bosses, you could be running scared forever, or worse."

Ella told all this to Stacey, who immediately hobbled down and turned the breaker off. Just as Dan was at the edge of the drive, he saw all the cabin lights go off. He turned off the car ignition and headlights and carefully walked the rest of the way to the back of the house with a crazed feeling. Thoughts ran through his head that maybe Ella and Stacey had become more than friends. Perhaps Marco had decided to side with her. Dan's temper was running wild as the rage inside him broke loose. His ego clouded his judgment. He could not let Ella slip out of his control. He'd teach her and Stacey who was in charge.

Chapter 58

CALL TO BLUFF

S itting at the hospital trying to help Billy bluff death proved a losing hand for Chase. This time around, the tall, dark gambler won. A second heart attack within a month was just too much, the doctor said. Chase knew better. Billy's heart had been broken for a long time. He hoped now he would be at peace. He would miss his friend and mentor. Over the past ten years, Billy had introduced him to a fine line in Vegas but helped keep Chase just over to the right. He stayed away from legal troubles but would always run into a few snags along the way. Meeting almost everyone connected to anyone and mastering the art of gambling and security within the casinos, or any building for that matter, kept him a sought-after man. Chase had become one to know in Vegas. He had it all, except someone with whom to enjoy the good life. Now, even his closest friend was taken from him.

Janie Blue had come into his life at a perfect moment. She was gone before he even knew what hit him. Now, he was sure she wanted nothing to do with him because of his association with Billy—a strange coincidence, or did she really play him? He would never know unless he asked her again. He fell for her enough to make sure she would be safe even if she hated him. Billy had spoken to every contact he knew until finding out who indeed ordered the hit by Marco. Finding out that it was actually her husband, Dan, made Chase crazy. How the hell did this new senatorial candidate from Washington carry so much clout?

Finding out that R. J. Davies, a political rival of Mac's, needed changes to policies made more sense. It explained why Ella was a necessary component to Dan's stability and likability. Any bad reputation at that time would have meant a sure loss of the election. Of course, no one knew that the hit was actually Chase O'Leary or that Billy would be involved. This strange turn of events was an embarrassment to Davies. They finally compromised to keep Dan Carmichael's issues quiet and use him as a puppet. This would ensure Ella/Janie's safety. Before Billy died, he made sure that if anything happened to Janie, it would launch an all-out war. If anything funny showed up, Davies's connections in Vegas would be severed. Marco was then called to follow orders to protect the politician's wife. The tides had changed as long as they could keep that maniac Dan under control. The more information Chase received on him, the sicker he felt for Janie. On the other hand, the more he found out about Janie/Ella, the more he fell for her. With each bit of information, he could not believe she had sought him out. What is meant to be may just be.

Chase called Blake with the sad news about Billy's death. They would have the wake in seven days at the Pioneer Bar. It would be a room full of very important people and would need to be somewhat secretive. He hoped Janie had read the letter and fully understood the depth of Billy's feelings. Once Billy knew she was alive, there was nothing else on his mind except her happy future. He thought she deserved to live a life that her mother, Eliza Jane, had never attained because of her untimely death. Lizzie had truly been Billy's soul mate, he thought. Unfortunately, Billy felt sure he had squelched her spirit in more than one way. He was never able to lift the burden of sadness until he met Janie. It did not go away, but Billy did feel he could make good somehow. Although he wanted desperately to meet Janie again and make her understand, death had a way of putting life in perspective. Chase would give her some space, and in the meantime, would stay in contact with Marco in place of Billy. Chase knew he had the resources to find a way to help her out of a near-impossible situation once things quieted down.

Chapter 59

COLD SILENCE

I f a pin dropped, Ella and Stacey would have heard it. They barely took shallow breaths as they heard a car's engine cut.

"Damn," said Stacey. "There is no way that could be Marco yet, and I definitely did not tell anyone I was here tonight. That means Dan saw the lights go out. We need to move, Ella. Let's stop acting like mute sitting ducks. I have pepper spray in my nightstand. I'll grab that. You grab the bat under my bed."

Ella wanted to laugh at the archaic weapons Stacey had at hand to protect herself, but she needed to focus. The pepper spray had probably been in the drawer for years, so who knew if it worked? She would absolutely take her chances with the bat. They split up. There was not a sound for minutes. It felt like an hour. The adrenaline rushed through them making them feel as if their veins would explode. Ella could hear her heart beating. Thirty seconds later, a window smashed in the direction of the kitchen. She heard Stacey make a run for it as if she could tackle the six-four assailant. Dan had definitely turned. Ella heard one single gunshot and slumped knowing that Stacey did not own a gun. She hid in a large chest, trying to muffle her soft crying. Footsteps continued to thump slowly through the house. As usual, Dan was not afraid. He always seemed to be in control and wanted to be the winner of every game. Ella would get angrier and angrier every damn time they played Monopoly; she was certain he would win because he cheated most of the time. He was much scarier after she had the accident. She was not sure whether he wanted to kill her or have sex. She tried to tell herself every time that it was just his way of securing an air of control.

As eerie silence filled the room, she thought he either left the room or was standing in front of her. She decided not to get trapped. Suddenly, she threw open the chest door. The trunk caught Dan's chin and he yelled, "You bitch, you will pay for this like your friend!"

At that, Ella swung without even looking. With all of her strength and anger, she put momentum behind the bat as if hitting a home run. She caught him in the head. The gun flew from his hand, and Dan hit the ground with a thud. As Ella looked at his lifeless body, the memories came flooding back. She shrank to the corner of the room and buried her head in her hands between her shaking knees. She was all alone again.

The lights were off as Marco maneuvered around Dan's car. There was not a sound. He hoped he was not too late. Marco kicked open the front door and immediately saw Stacey lying motionless on the ground. She had been shot.

He yelled, "Ella, Dan, we need to talk! This dinner is more important than any argument." He hoped Dan's warped mind would respond to a brush with reality.

Nobody answered, so Marco kept walking. He understood his orders to protect Ella, but he also realized how far they had come with Dan. His bosses wanted changes made in their favor and had spent a lot of time and money to get this prick elected. Somehow, this needed to happen or somebody would pay. He made his way through the house, silently checking every door and corner until he got to the bedroom where Ella sat huddled in the corner next to Dan's body.

This was definitely a dilemma. He wanted to protect and hide Ella while he blamed this incident on her friend, but knew he needed to come up with another plan fast.

"So, you have thrown my plan to the wind," he said, picking Ella up off the floor. He wanted to give the girl a hug but knew it would be inappropriate. Instead, he sat her on the bed and told her, "It's okay. He was an asshole. I have an idea, but we need to get you out of here right away. It is a good thing this cabin is pretty isolated. I did not see anyone on the last few roads getting here, so I doubt Dan did either."

"Stacey? Is she dead? I heard the shot and then nothing," she asked in a daze.

When Marco came in, he had stepped over her body but did not stop, as the main priority handed down from his boss was to protect Ella, and keep Dan working at his job. Well, this would be a difficult one to explain. However, Marco was good at cleaning up and fixing even the worst "messes."

"I don't think she made it, Ella. She must have surprised him, and it didn't look as if he thought before he shot. I am sorry." He put one arm around her to lead her out of the house. "Time to go. Now. This will get ugly soon if I don't move on this."

Ella was in shock and her brain felt like it was in a thick fog. Her entire family was now dead. Stacey was like her sister, not just a best friend. Seeing her body on the floor, Ella ran toward her and knelt down. She held her hand. It felt very warm. Marco started walking around her body as he thought he saw a slight movement.

"Hey, I think she may be alive—barely. Check her pulse."

Ella frantically checked her pulse and put her head to her chest, listening for a faint heartbeat. As they turned her body over, both noticed the bullet had not hit any organs but had taken a chunk out of her side. That is why there was so much blood.

Elated to have something to be relieved about, however dismal,

Ella let out a small sigh. "She must have hit her head and fell unconscious. Let's lay her on the couch."

Stacey came to, moaning in pain and holding her head. They had cleaned the wound, and Ella was applying pressure using a dish towel to stop the bleeding.

"Who do you two think you are, doctors?" Even in a near-death situation, Stacey could be sarcastic. She moved the towel and Ella's hand, saying, "I think the bullet went straight through. There's not enough blood for it to have hit anything. It's my head that worries me. Ella, can you grab my bag? It's in the bathroom under the sink."

Being a doctor held some advantages in crises such as this. Stacey would be fine. Marco told Ella and Stacey he had changed his mind. He needed them to stay at the cabin, but he must take Dan's body with him.

After thinking for a long moment, he told them confidently, "I have a plan."

Chapter 60

CROSSROADS

Another day, another funeral. The life of Ella Carmichael seemed jinxed. It was time for her to start over. Wanting to pass out on her bed after a long, guilt-ridden day playing the sad, grieving wife had worn her out. It was easy to grieve, as she had not done enough of it for the others she lost. Now, she felt a strange emptiness. At the same time, she was free from Dan. Almost. She would carry the guilt of his death for the rest of her life, yet she knew he would have killed her that night without thinking twice.

Her clothes from two days ago still lay strewn across her chair. As she picked up the parka to hang it up, she noticed an envelope sticking out of the pocket. It was addressed to "Janie." She had forgotten that Chase had put it there when she had dismissed him so poorly. She sat in the chair to read the note, but was surprised at the contents as soon as she began.

Dear Janie,

I hope someday you can forgive me, although I know you will never forget the night of your mother's death. I was filled with jealousy, rage, and cocaine, the very drug I had started selling. Not an excuse, but the reality. No matter what measures I take to change my life and future actions, I can never take back that night. I know that.

Eliza Jane (Lizzie) was the most amazing, beautiful, and witty woman I have ever met. She was the true love of my life. Just as she was that to me, you were the love and light of her life. You two were the only family I had really known, and I lost everything that evening. I searched for you for years on end, hoping to hear you were okay and to help out anonymously any way I could. There was no trace of you. This seemed crazy to me because of the connections I have made. I am sorry to hear of the loss of your mother and recently your father. I will do everything in my power to ensure your safety and protection now and after my death.

I have included the deeds to several properties and some other items that I feel should belong to you. One is the Pioneer Bar. It was your mother's favorite place to go. She even took you there as a child. She created a huge adventure in the old "ghost town" for you. We had all kinds of tricks set up there. When I go there, sometimes I feel her presence. Who knows, maybe the legend is true. I hope you accept these properties and make them your own.

If you have this letter, we probably won't get a chance to talk again. Although not under the best of circumstances, meeting you was like seeing your mother again. You have her beauty, grace, and feisty attitude. If Chase has such strong feelings about you, then you must be something very special. May you find what you're looking for and then some.

Yours truly,
Billy

Ella sat in disbelief. In the next instant, she knew her next move. After making phone calls to Marco and Stacey and putting together some clothes, Ella drove up to her parents' home on the island. It was now her home again. She walked through the entire house, touched every bedpost, faucet, and doorknob. Memories of her childhood came flooding back in waves. Finally, she grabbed the keys on the yellow smiley face key ring from the kitchen drawer and walked to the old barn where the cars were stored. Sure enough, her hunch was right. Her father had completely fixed the MG. She looked beautiful again. It was as if he did it for her mother, Kate.

After opening the doors to the barn, Ella jumped in the little convertible, started the engine, and promised the car she would take a new route this time. Parking outside, she transferred her things to the MG and parked her Land Rover inside the barn. Ella was ready for a new beginning.

Opening the trunk, she noticed a bunch of old cassettes, which she had not seen before. She put her bags in and took all of the cassettes into the car with her. She would need some music for the road trip. Looking through the stack of great old tunes, Ella grabbed the Simon and Garfunkel cassette marked "BEST" in the corner in red permanent marker. She knew they were her dad's favorite. She hoped the cassette player still worked. Pushing it in the slot felt so familiar. With a little patience, she fast-forwarded until she got to "Homeward Bound." Would she really be going home? There was something special about her destination. Her biggest fear was that Chase would refuse her. Perhaps like the song, her love would lie waiting silently for her.

Chapter 61

HOMEWARD BOUND

I t was a beautiful day leaving Washington—a perfect day by which to remember her family. Nothing surprised her best friend. Stacey pulled up just as she was about to start her journey.

"Seriously, you thought you could leave without a huge hug good-bye from *me*! Afraid I would talk you out of it?"

Smiling a wide smile for the first time in months, Ella jumped out of the car and ran to Stacey. "Promise to visit soon? Don't ever forget that blood bond we share," she said, giggling like a teenager.

"Never." She got serious for a moment and pressed her lips together, forming a sad smile. "I really believe this is the right thing for you to do, Ella. Let all of the press and talk die down for a while. You may not want to come back, except to visit me, of course. Oh, by the way, Marco thought it better to lay low and wait for the dust to settle also. He sent a note to my office asking me to tell you he'd be in contact and to stay safe. That means no country roads for you, Ella."

"Got it. Love you, Stace." With that they hugged. Then, Ella jumped in the car, cranked the top down, and drove away. She did not think she'd be back for a long while.

She spent the night in a small hotel along the way. Before leaving the hotel the next day, Ella slipped on a simple black shift dress. Although she did not want to arrive too disheveled, she could not resist the urge to keep the top down the last few hours of the drive. The sun was hot and felt great. Her hair was tousled and wild, but it made her feel carefree and happy like the first time she remembered coming here. She drove into the dusty parking lot slowly and parked. There were about fifteen cars parked out front. Ella walked around to the back of the bar and tentatively opened the door. She was late to the wake, but no one noticed. There was a lot of cheering, clinking of shot glasses, and storytelling going on. She stood quietly in the shadowed background. Her black hair, tanned skin, and dark dress helped her blend right in.

It was an entertaining wake, to say the least. She wanted to pay her respects to Billy. His letter had struck a chord with Ella. She needed forgiveness as a sense of freedom for herself and a redemption for Billy. Seeing Blake looking around as he was getting another round of drinks for everyone, Ella saw him focus in on her and smile. He looked as if he were about to come talk to her, but she motioned for him to stay and put her finger to her mouth to silence him. Blake nodded in understanding, and the wake concluded with one last toast.

Just as she had come in through the back door, Ella gently closed the door behind her as she left. She was not sure who all the men were, but recognized O'Shea, Jax, and, of course, Chase. She did not want to leave without seeing him. Closing her eyes for a moment, she remembered their first, intense kiss. A handful of men walked outside, but she saw only one. Blake asked Chase to grab some retro CDs he had made for the event from his car. He hoped Janie had not left yet and Chase would bump into her. His friend had been hit hard first by her rejection and then by Billy's death. Everyone needed closure—or maybe another try.

At first, Chase did not see her as he walked toward Blake's car. She was leaning against the front of his Jeep, watching him longingly.

Taking a risk, she called, "Chase!"

His heart skipped. He'd know her slightly raspy voice anywhere. As he turned around, he saw something silver in the air, sparking light from the sun. He caught the small bracelet easily. In his hand, he held the delicate slot machine and ace charms now connected to a small silver chain. When he looked up, Janie was tentatively walking toward him with a beautiful, one-of-a-kind smile on her face.

Taking quick, long strides, he was in front of her within seconds. Not hesitating, Chase picked her up and kissed her tenderly on the lips. Next, he put her down and, holding her hands, stretched out her arms to admire her as if making sure she was not a mirage. It had been a long day after all. No words passed, but they were not needed.

Interrupting them, the back door flew open and Blake came running over. Without pleasantries, he yelled, "The Hotel Du Monde is up in flames!" Back inside the bar, they turned on the television and saw a huge explosion being replayed on the news. Some of the men began singing loudly and drunkenly to the song "Light My Fire" by the Doors.

Janie couldn't help but wonder, *Which door will open next?*

The End . . .

for Now

ACKNOWLEDGMENTS

As the saying goes, it takes a village!

This journey started with the intent to write about the injustices of insurance companies after we suffered a total loss of our new home from a terrible fire. At the same time, my mom was in Las Vegas fighting for her life against a beast of a brain tumor, from which she sadly passed a month later.

I met an accomplished author, James Strauss, at our local coffee shop. He encouraged me *not* to write about my angst, which was too raw and depressing then, but rather to create a healthy escape through fiction. Thank you for guiding me through the process over lattes!

Thanks to that advice, I diverted my deep frustrations and depressing thoughts into creating intense, viscous characters and weaving them together to form this fast-paced romantic thriller.

To my friends and family, I love you for pushing me to write with your enthusiastic comments after reading my very unedited pages. Susan Alison, you are a rock star whose support and conviction that Janie Blue needed to "have a voice" pushed me to the next level.

Lisa Burwell (my amazing friend and owner of *VIE* magazine) and her talented team at The Idea Boutique have been instrumental in getting *Janie Blue* to the finish line! From editing to creating a stunning, symbolic cover and preparing to publish, they added a fresh perspective and exuded positivity through every step! You are so appreciated.

The time is here to spin the wheel or play a hand, and I hope everyone who reads *Janie Blue* gets lost in this story for a while and enjoys the ride. Thank you!

ABOUT THE AUTHOR

SUZY ACCOLA is a debut author living in Santa Rosa Beach, Florida, on the white-sand beaches of the Emerald Coast. She is a wife, mother of three, dog mom, and owner of a busy design showroom and boutique focusing on interior surfaces and favorite finds. She and her husband work together as a design-build team and have a lot of fun in the process! Her passion is crafting beautiful stories, whether through words on a page or finishes in a home. Creativity feeds her soul and gives her the energy to open new doors, face tough challenges, and greet each day as a blessing.

Janie Blue is available on Amazon.com.

Author photo by BRENNA KNEISS